WATCH CITY

Watch City

ADAM MATSON

Adam Matson

Contents

1	Watch City	1
2	Scream Queen	13
3	Sertraline Dreams	24
4	A Dark North Territory	37
5	Coyotes	58
6	Effigy	84
7	Just the Usual Horses	107
8	Mercy Kill	124
9	Odd-Numbered Streets	142
10	Saucy Jack	159

11	The Clearing	189
12	The Human Word-Processor	197
13	Toesies	205

Acknowledgements 213
About The Author 214

Chapter 1

Watch City

Mary stood in front of the window in her underwear and stared out at the Charles River, her cell phone pressed to her ear. This was Roland's favorite view of her, and he prayed she would stand still long enough for him to finish his deed. Roland's condo was two stories above Mary's, his windows perpendicular to hers, offering him the view of her living room. He turned out the lights, dropped his pants, and stroked himself as he watched her.

Afterwards he retreated to his bedroom and tried to sleep, but could not. Fantasies of Mary lubricated his mind.

At 35, he should have had a girlfriend. He should have been married. His sister June, three years younger, was married, had two kids, a husband, a pretty good job. The clock was ticking.

Roland did not have had a wife, children, a dog, or any meaningful social connections. But he did have a rewarding job, repairing computer, which had bought him his condo in the old Waltham Watch Factory, in Waltham, Massachusetts, the Watch City. That was how he met Mary. A storm surge fried the USB port on her laptop. She found Roland on the internet, remarked how convenient it was that they lived in the same building. When he went to her apartment and fixed her computer, he saw through her living room window the light above in his own apartment.

It was late afternoon, and Mary pranced in front of the window showcasing a runway of underwear. Roland pushed his couch against his window and crouched behind it, watching her. His heart sank when The Boyfriend showed up. Roland had seen the boyfriend several times, did not know his name, but called him Chet because he was thick and muscular, and smirked rather than smiled. Roland hated him.

Mary kissed Chet in front of the window. Then she grabbed her purse and they left together.

Roland's ex-girlfriend Rachel had left him three years earlier. The only serious girlfriend of his life, she had admired his ability to fix and improve machines. He had rebuilt her toaster to cook bread more uniformly, rewired her cable box to open up hundreds of channels. But Rachel complained that they never went out, always just sat at home watching TV. She told Roland that he was too much like a machine, performing the commands of a boyfriend without any passion or humanity.

After Mary left with Chet, Roland thought about going out. There was no reason he couldn't walk to the bars. His apartment was a suffocating place, hemorrhaging empty fantasies. Mary's window was like a dead eye staring up at him.

Roland locked his apartment and walked downstairs to the lobby. He almost left the building and went outside, but instead followed the staircase down to the basement. The buzz of street traffic above and the rush of the river outside faded to silence. Roland stood in a long corridor lined with closed doors. One by one he tried to open them, but found each of them locked. Toward the end of the hallway, he grasped a doorknob and it turned, surprising him as he stumbled into a dark room filled with crates.

Roland wrenched the lids off a few of the crates, found them to be filled with thousands of tiny watch components.

Then he noticed the tiny door of an old combination safe on the wall. He twisted the lock, and it gave a little, so he wrenched it hard counter-clockwise. The lock snapped in a puff of dust.

Inside the safe was a simple hand-crafted wooden box with gilded trim. Only a small latch secured its lock, and Roland easily snapped it.

The box contained a simple gold watch, with white Roman numerals on the stark black face. It had a single hand, frozen on one of the sixty little minute marks of the hour. The other hand was missing, but Roland could fix that.

It was 12:42 AM when the light came on in Mary's apartment. Roland knew the time exactly because he checked his new watch. He had affixed two tiny hands to the face of the clock, one for minutes, one for seconds. When he wound the crown, the watch whispered to life, its tick like a tiny heartbeat.

Mary and the boyfriend settled onto the couch, started making out. Roland shut off his light and watched them. The presence of Chet filled him with jealousy. He wanted

Mary to himself, could not complete his need with the boyfriend there. Mary climbed onto the boyfriend's lap, and Roland watched with murderous hatred as they thrust against each other.

When it was over Roland felt empty and alone. He should have jerked off anyway, to spite them. Why should the boyfriend have all the fun? It was a moment Roland would take back if he could.

Suddenly he had an idea. Curious and desperate, he cranked back the crown of his watch, winding the minute hand back twelve minutes.

He found himself sitting by the window again, staring out at the river. Mary's light flicked on, and he frowned down at it. Had they left and come back? Or had he really reset the scene, erased twelve minutes and rebooted time?

He stared dumbly at Mary and Chet as they fucked again, exactly as they had before. Roland suppressed his panic and this time accomplished the goal he had set out to achieve.

The thrill of the stolen orgasm passed in a microsecond. He felt neither ashamed nor jealous, but contemplated Mary's window with a clear head. He had another idea: he could deprive the boyfriend of the experience altogether.

Again, he reset the watch by twelve minutes. This time he grabbed a handful of the cogs he had taken from the crate in the basement, turned off his living room light, and opened his window. He waited until Mary was just about to climb onto the boyfriend's lap, then he hurled the cogs at her window.

Mary and the boyfriend stood up and stared confusedly outside. They spoke briefly, not looking at each other. Chet reached out to touch her shoulder, but she shrugged him off, covering herself and retreating from the window.

Roland snuck off to his bedroom with the watch, fell asleep with a grin on his face.

The following night Mary whirled around her apartment in full display. She wore the red lace underwear- Roland's favorite. Tonight she did not seem to be getting ready to go out, but instead appeared to be setting up a romantic dinner in. Roland did not want to endure another session of aggressive love-making. He would not be left clutching himself in burning jealousy.

He thought of his watch. If he could head off the boyfriend, he could sneak down to Mary's condo, surprise her, have her all to himself. She was already nearly naked. He could sweet talk her in the doorway. If he said something stupid or off-putting, he could simply rewind his watch and try again. He could knock on her door a hundred times.

Roland ran downstairs to Mary's apartment. He should have brought her a gift, but there was nothing handy. He did not want to wind the watch back half an hour and run to the store for flowers and chocolates. That might ruin his nerve.

He knocked on her door. There was a long moment before any response came from within. Roland wondered what the hell he was doing.

He saw a shadow beneath the door frame.

"Hello?" came Mary's voice from the other side of the door.

"Mary? It's Roland. Roland Herkimer. From upstairs."

There was no response.

"The computer guy."

"Oh!"

Mary slowly opened the door. She was wearing a bathrobe. Roland realized she had probably checked him out through the peephole. This wasn't going well already. She stared at him expectantly.

"I was just walking by your apartment," he said. "And I remembered your laptop. Just wanted to check in and see how everything was working."

"Everything's fine," Mary said. "Thanks, Roland. Thanks for asking."

"All right," Roland said. He stood in the doorway. *Abort, abort, abort.* He heard the ding of the elevator, saw Mary glance past him.

Roland touched the crown of his watch and rolled it back a few ticks.

Back in his room, he watched Mary rushing around in her underwear, setting the table for dinner. He would not go back down there again. He stared at her curiously. She did not seem to notice that he had reversed time.

Roland slumped onto his couch, tried not to think of Mary, tried to watch his television, but nothing interested him. He went back to the window and saw that now the happy couple was sharing a candle-lit dinner by the window. The boyfriend was dressed in khakis and a polo shirt. Mary was still wearing only the underwear, tantalizing Chet with smiles, thrusting her cleavage toward him. Roland's head filled with hot blood. Rachel had done something similar with him once. She had answered her apartment door naked, invited him inside. He had just stood there dumbly, trying act cool. That was a night he wished he could rewind to.

Roland decided to sabotage Mary's dinner. He picked up his phone and dialed her number, which he had saved to his contacts. She did not answer on the first set of rings, so he dialed again, and she picked up right away.

"Hello?" She sounded anxious.

"Yes, this is the Waltham Police Department," Roland said, lowering his voice an octave. "We're just calling to inform you, ma'am, that there is a sexual predator in your neighborhood, and we advise you not to leave your home."

"What?"

Roland had no idea what he was saying. He did not want to scare her. He just wanted to spoil the dinner.

"Who is it?" he heard the boyfriend ask.

"They said it was the police," Mary said.

"What do they want?"

"Something about a sexual predator-"

"What?"

"But it's so weird," Mary said. "The number on the caller ID said 'Roland Computer Guy.'"

Roland's blood froze. He never thought of the caller ID. Was he losing his mind?

"Who the hell is that?" Chet asked.

"You know that guy who fixed my computer?" Mary said. "He lives in the building, so I kept his number. Hello?" she said into the phone.

"What the fuck does he want?" Chet asked, and Roland heard the sound a chair scraping against the floor.

He hung up. "Goddammit!" He slammed his phone against his couch. Then he realized that Chet was probably coming up to his apartment right now. With a shaky hand he twisted back the crown of his watch.

Adrenaline coursing through his veins, Roland turned the clock back further than he intended. Now it was an hour earlier. He was sitting by the window, watching Mary set up the dinner table again. He punched the glass of his window. The blow opened up a bloody gash on his knuckle. He turned the watch back thirty seconds. The gash vanished.

Taking a book of matches and a newspaper, he ran into the corridor, snuck into the stairwell. He lit the newspaper and tossed it into a trash can below the smoke alarm.

Minutes later he heard sirens approaching the Watch Factory. He hurried out into the hallway. The air was thick with smoke. What the hell had happened? It was just supposed to be a trash cash fire. Flames billowed from the stairwell. Roland ran down the corridor and took the emergency stairs to the ground floor. Heart racing, he sprinted outside. A crowd stood in the parking lot across the street from his building. He saw Mary, standing in her bathrobe, staring up at the old watch factory in terror, the boyfriend's arms wrapped around her.

Roland turned and saw the whole roof of the watch factory on fire. He cursed himself as the fire engines screamed up Crescent Street. Firefighters rushed toward the building with their hoses.

"Don't bother," Roland whispered, and he cranked back his watch.

This time he would do it right. The boyfriend had thwarted him at every turn, and so should be subtracted from the equation.

Roland waited in the shadows at the far end of the Watch Factory. It was autumn, and darkness came early. He hid behind a dumpster, clutching a carving knife from the bachelor cooking set his sister had once given him for Christmas.

There was no going back after this. No returning to the nights at the window jacking off in pathetic, wallowing jealousy. Mary would be his, and if she wouldn't have him, he would keep tweaking the watch until she came around.

A sedan pulled into a parking space next to the Watch Factory. Roland saw the boyfriend behind the wheel. He watched as Chet or Chaz fixed his appearance in the rearview mirror, straightened his hair, sipped off a bottle of something. Then he turned off the car and stepped out into the night.

Roland dashed across the parking lot with the knife raised. Chet walked calmly ahead of him, as if in slow motion, and Roland felt like he was in a dream, running through sand.

"Chet," he grunted when he was only a few feet from the man. Chet turned with a confused look on his face.

Roland plunged the knife deep into the boyfriend's throat. Blood poured from the wound. The color drained from Chet's face as he clutched his neck, gasping for air. Roland stabbed him again, this time in the base of the skull, and he saw the man's eyes roll back in his head as he collapsed to the pavement.

For a moment all Roland could hear was his own loud, hot breathing. His vision had narrowed to a tunnel. The knife trembled in his hand, and he realized he was crying.

Terrified, he grabbed Chet's blood-soaked shirt and dragged the body into the shadows. The corpse was heavier than he expected, like dragging a tarp full of wet leaves.

Roland poured sweat as he heaved the corpse down to the edge of the river. He flung the carving knife into the black water, then dragged Chet's body in. He tried to push the body under, but it would not sink. Instead he pushed it outward, toward the current. The body inched away. Roland staggered back onto the shore, sat down in the grass beside his apartment building. He could not believe what he had just done. His mind swirled with visions of the dam at the old mill downstream, its current running red with blood.

He could not do this. Could not go through with it. He may have been lonely and desperate, a recluse, as Rachel had said, but he was not a murderer. He reached for the watch and cranked back the crown.

Nothing happened. Panic seized his chest. He twisted the crown backward, forward, wrenching it first clockwise, then counter-clockwise, but still he remained sitting beside the river, his clothes soaking wet, his vision blurred with tears. He slammed the watch against the brick wall of the building and felt a shudder as it shattered. The glass of the face cracked like a spider's web. The hands stood perfectly still.

He awoke in his bed, and it was morning. He was still wearing his clothes and shoes from the night before, but they were dry, and bore no dirt or grime or any traces of blood.

The murder came back to him like a punch. He ran to the bathroom and threw up.

No one would ever believe him about the watch. He was insane, that's all, had gone insane from years of self-imposed isolation. He had murdered Mary's boyfriend, Chet or Chuck. He should confess and then everything would be fixed. They would lock him away in prison or a mental institution, somewhere official, and someone in authority would explain everything to him.

Yes, he decided. He would confess. And get help. Everything would become clear.

He walked downstairs to Mary's apartment, wondering if the police had found the corpse. Maybe they were pulling it from the drainage pipes down at the dam.

Mary answered the door on his third knock. She was wearing a bathrobe and her hair was messy, but she smiled at him and said: "Roland? What are you doing here?"

He was surprised that she remembered his name.

"I'm so sorry," he said, tears welling up in his eyes. "I murdered Chet."

Her smile vanished. She took a step backward. "What?"

"Chet," he said. "Or Chuck. I don't- your boyfriend. I'm so sorry." He cried into his hands. "I killed him last night."

Mary took another step backward, her expression now utterly confused. "Rob?" she called.

Roland looked up, heard footsteps in the condo. The boyfriend appeared, wearing sweatpants and a tee shirt, holding a spatula. Roland smelled bacon cooking.

"What did you just say?" Mary asked Roland.

His blood froze. The boyfriend was alive. Rob was his name, not Chet, and he was alive. Roland stumbled backwards. He glanced at his watch. The hands were frozen and unmoving.

"What did he say?" Rob asked.

"He said he murdered someone," Mary said.

"Are you for real, guy?" Rob said, stepping out into the hall.

Roland had no idea what was going on. He was too scared to be relieved that Rob was alive. He turned and ran down the hall.

"Mary, call the police," he heard Rob say, and the door to Mary's condo slammed shut.

Back in his apartment, Roland locked the door and slumped against the wall. He stared at the watch, afraid to touch the crown. Now he knew why someone long ago had dismantled it and locked it deep beneath the old factory.

He did not know how much time had passed when he heard pounding on his door.

"Roland Herkimer?" a rough-sounding voice called.

Roland heard the jingle of metal. Keys, he thought. Or handcuffs.

"This is the police, Mr. Herkimer. We need to talk to you."

"Open the door, sir," another voice demanded.

Roland took a deep breath. The terrible pounding continued. The voices got louder. He covered his ears.

His only potential escape was the watch. He grabbed the crown and twisted, hoping that somehow it would take him back to a better time, before Chet/Rob was a corpse drifting down the river, when Mary was his tantalizing beauty, and Roland had cast a yearning eye over Watch City.

Chapter 2

Scream Queen

Los Angeles sparkled below us like creation itself, as we stood like gods against the railing of the overlook.

Danny and I decided to drive up Mulholland one night for no other reason than that there's no other road quite like it. A twisting mountain passage with big houses and lush trees, hairpin turns and steep canyons. The city shines around you, boundless.

Danny had moved to LA to become an actor, against his parents' wishes, and I had moved there because he said it was awesome, against my parents' wishes.

"This is the street where Brando lived, dude," Danny said when we were back in the car, winding our way through the mountains. "I mean, he actually *lived* here."

So far he had not landed any significant roles in television or film. He was paying his dues, doing background and extra work, trying to accrue enough hours to join the union.

His biggest part so far was playing a college student in a UCLA promotional video.

"You want extra money, Russ, you should come with me," Danny said. "You're Asian."

"Asian." We laughed. "Not Chinese?"

"It's all the same to them."

Danny Ma. Russell Chang. Both of us born in Concord, Massachusetts. About as Chinese as crab rangoons.

"It sucks, we don't even know martial arts," Danny said. "We could be background Yakuza."

"They never taught us to fight in Advanced Calculus."

We were a long way from high school. Danny and I, and Grace Yi, and Hideki Matsumoto, had been so smart they'd created a special math class for us. Of course, right? Grace was at Yale Medical School now. Hideki was getting his Master's at M.I.T.

"Last month I worked background as a programmer on *Silicon Valley*," Danny said, rocking in the passenger seat. "My parents were so excited when I told them. They thought I'd gotten a job *as* a programmer, and *moved* to Silicon Valley."

"My parents think I'm out here looking at grad schools," I said.

Really I was majoring in Los Angeles. One thing I loved about LA was that you could be listening to your favorite band while driving to a restaurant, then sit down to dinner, and the singer from that band might be at the table next to you. Then the next day you might go surfing out in Malibu. In January.

"Jack Nicholson lives around here somewhere," Danny said.

We rounded a sharp turn, and in the street light ahead of us we saw a white woman running naked down the road.

Instinctively I slowed down, and Danny turned off the radio.

"What do you think is up with this?" he asked.

"I don't know."

In any other city this might be The Weirdest Thing You Ever Saw, but in LA it was about a 6.5 out of 10.

I cruised past the woman, and we both turned to look at her. Her eyes were so wide we could see the whites, and she was screaming loud enough to drown out my engine.

"Dude, pull over."

I eased to a stop. She ran toward us, a red, naked mirage in my tail lights.

"What do we do?" Danny asked.

"Well," I said, but I had nothing. I put the car in park and we got out, left the doors open and the engine running. The woman looked to be about our age, mid-twenties.

"Help me!" she cried, her voice harsh and out of breath. "They're chasing me!"

I held out my hands to either offer help or keep her at bay. Danny stood there with his mouth hanging open.

"It's okay," I said, in a voice that did not sound like my own.

"Please help me! They're chasing me!"

"Who's chasing you?"

"I don't know!" Her whole body rippled with tremors. She held her shaking hands against her chest. "I met them at a club- they said they were producers- they asked if I wanted to hang out- I went-"

Her words sputtered out like stray bullets.

"They put something in my drink- I think they put something in my drink- suddenly they were pulling my clothes off- and I just ran! Oh, God, please help me!"

"Okay," I said again. "It's okay."

I looked at Danny. His face was pale. In the distance we could hear the roar of the city.

"Where the fuck are you?"

A man's voice cried out in the darkness, somewhere above us.

The girl released a high-pitched shriek. I stood frozen still. She screamed again.

"She's down on the fuckin' road!"

Another voice, older, rougher.

"Let's get out of here," Danny whispered.

I grabbed the girl's arm and pulled her toward the car. Opened the back door, and she jumped in.

Behind us we heard the squealing tires of a car.

"Oh, Jesus," Danny said.

The girl screamed again.

"It's okay, calm down!" I cried.

She twisted around, staring out the back window. "Hurry! Go!"

I hit the gas, but Mulholland was not a race course. Going over 30 was a bad idea.

The road rose steeply and we grumbled uphill. A car came the other way and I swerved suddenly, riding the ditch. There was no guardrail and a steep drop beside us. Danny closed his eyes.

I braked and took a deep breath. We crept around a hairpin turn, cruised into a straightaway. I floored it again. Climbed higher into the hills. Frantically checked the rearview. The girl began to moan.

"Oh, god, it's them...."

I turned and saw headlights behind us. Not right behind, but several turns back, and a couple hundred feet below. Far enough that I could lose them.

"Just go, man," Danny said. "Don't look back."

"Please go faster," the girl said.

"I'm going as fast as I can!"

I stepped on it, jerking the wheel like an arcade game, the car growling, lurching, steering wheel shaking. The trees vanished beside us and we saw the San Fernando Valley sprawling in the canyon below.

I scanned the road for a driveway, a turn, anything.

"Call the fucking cops," I said to Danny.

He stared at his phone. "No reception up here."

I threw mine at him.

"Nothing," he said. "Shit."

The headlights flickered in the rearview, dipping in and out of the darkness like a winking eye. The girl started to cry.

Ahead I saw a side street, winding uphill, no street lights, black. I jammed on the breaks and swerved into the turn, gunned it up the hill, nearly lost it on another sharp turn, stopped suddenly in the parking space of a "scenic overlook." Shut off the car.

"Nobody move."

Through the trees we could see Mulholland below us. I stared at the black road, not breathing. Danny leaned forward and craned his neck for a view. The girl clutched her face, sucking back tears.

A moment later a car went by. We saw the red flash of tail lights and a bolt of ice shot through my heart.

But the tail lights vanished, bleeding away. We did not move. The night air was hot and still.

"I think we're okay," I said eventually.

"Where does this road go?" Danny asked.

I had no idea.

From the backseat I could hear the girl's teeth chattering. I turned around, averted my eyes from her nakedness.

"There's a bathing suit and towel back there," I said, pointing randomly.

She fished around in the dark and found my bathing suit, pulled it on. She wrapped the towel around her shoulders. She sat there quaking, mouth moving but no words coming out. Eyes bleary now, dazed.

"We should find a police station," Danny said.

"I think we need to get back on Mulholland," I said.

"No," said the girl.

"I have no idea where we are."

One turn and lost. I started the car and crept around in a slow circle, headed back down the slope. Stopped at the intersection.

"Back the way we came?" Danny asked.

"That's a long way," I said. "We're not far from the 405. Maybe a couple of miles."

I turned back onto Mulholland. Now we were heading the same direction as the car that had been following us. I saw no tail lights ahead.

I drove slowly, normally, fingers gripping the wheel, heart pounding. The turns were sudden and pitch black, every curve a possible collision. We drove for a couple of miles. No freeway.

Danny kept checking his phone.

"Signal?"

"No."

"What's your name?" I asked the girl in the back.

"B- Briana."

"I'm Russ, this is Dan. We're going to take you to the police."

Easier said than done. We passed several roads, some of them labeled, others not, leading either up or down into darkness. The city bubbled on the horizon like lava.

"Oh God...." Briana groaned.

"Slow down, man."

A Porsche or a Ferrari, some ungodly fast LA car, had stopped in the middle of the lane, engine running, tail lights like red eyes glaring at us.

"That's their car," Briana said.

"Get down," I told her. "Just get way down, on the floor. Don't look up."

I pulled into the oncoming lane. The sports car's driver's window rolled down and a young man with a blonde beard and curly hair leaned out. "Hey!" he cried.

"Don't stop," Danny said.

"It's cool," I said. "They don't know who we are."

The man waved. Clearly wanted us to stop. I rolled to a stop, rolled down Danny's window.

"Hey, man," the man said, grinning, smoking a butt. "Hey, dudes, listen, this is so weird, but did you see a naked chick back there on the road? Like running? We kinda lost her."

"No," I said. "Back where on the road?"

Danny said nothing.

"Yeah, fuck," the man said, half-laughing. "She just jumped out of our car, man. Crazy fuckin' bitch. Give 'em a little E and it's like... you know what I mean?"

"Yeah," I said. "Didn't see anybody. Sorry."

I started to drive away.

"Hey!" he called after us.

I picked up speed. The Porsche revved to life.

"Shit," Danny said, rolling up his window. "What if they have a fuckin' gun?"

Briana started crying again in the back.

"I don't know, man, are they coming?"

The Porsche roared behind us. I stepped on the gas, taking the turns way too fast, careening through the night. We passed another oncoming car and missed it by inches.

The Porsche caught up to us in about thirty seconds. Rode our tail.

"Russ, he's gonna hit us!" Danny cried.

"Please don't stop!" Briana wailed. She sat up, saw the headlights behind us, and let out another quaking scream.

"Keep your head down!" I shouted.

But they definitely saw her now. The Porsche inched closer. Its headlights vanished in my rearview and I could now see the outlines of two heads.

Suddenly I was angry. They wanted to run us off the road. I would not let them fuck up my car. I eased off the gas.

"What are you doing?" Danny asked.

"Trying not to get us killed."

"Go fucking faster!" Briana shrieked.

I ignored them both. I had a plan. We passed a sign for the 405 and I felt a pinch of relief. Around the next turn the road straightened out, and I saw the freeway onramp. The 405 planed below us, blasting north and south like a runway.

I slowed the car to a stop, a hundred yards from the onramp.

"Russ, man, what the hell are you doing?"

Briana's crying turned to heaving sobs. She curled up in a ball and buried her face in the seat cushion. I watched the rearview mirror, waiting.

"Don't move," I whispered.

The Porsche sat about fifteen feet behind us, engine chugging, high beams burning into our car. I squinted into the side view, watching the driver's door.

"Come on...."

The door opened. A man stepped out, and started walking toward us.

"Oh, shit, Russ, they're coming." Danny squirmed in his seat.

I tried to see if the man was holding a gun, or any weapon, but it was too dark to see. Foot on the break, I shifted into Drive.

The man was two feet from my window, his buddy flanking us on Danny's side. I floored the accelerator and we rocketed toward the onramp. Eyes darting between the exit and the rearview, I saw the two men standing in the road, visibly surprised. They hesitated for maybe five seconds, then turned and ran back to their car.

Just enough time for us to make the onramp. I leaned hard on the wheel and punched the gas, tires squealing, the car drifting into the long turn. No headlights behind us. The onramp straightened, melted into the freeway and I blasted between the oncoming cars. No turn signal. In a split second we were a ghost on the freeway, one of a thousand anonymous cars.

In the rearview I saw the Porsche pull onto the highway behind us, but it was too far back. LA traffic hemmed it in, a long, moving fence, impenetrable.

"Both of you get down," I said, and Danny and Briana ducked.

I drove the speed limit, pulled into the right lane and put an eighteen-wheeler beside me. Glancing out the side window, I saw the Porsche haul ass two lanes over, flying by, a Hail Mary sailing down the road toward the city.

"Adios, amigos," I whispered.

We got off at Sunset, headed toward Westwood. Danny pulled up the GPS on his phone and guided us to a police station. Nobody was following us now.

"I have some more clothes in the trunk," I told Briana, and when we pulled into the police station I got them for her.

About a month later I told this story to a customer at the bar I worked at, and he said it might make a cool screenplay. He was a producer or something. I thought about it for about two days, even called the police station to speak to the detective.

"Never heard back from her," the detective said. "She had no idea who they were or where they took her, so there's nothing more we can do."

He sounded annoyed, as if the whole night on Mulholland had been some charade Briana and Danny and I had cooked up for kicks.

I let it drop.

But Los Angeles has a way of taking weird to the next level. About two months after the incident Danny was at a casting call on the Sony lot for a horror movie. He was auditioning for a role as an extra who died horribly. The scene called for a whole mob of people to die horribly.

As Danny told it to me later, he was waiting around to meet the casting director, and in the conference room where the reading was he heard this blood-curdling woman's scream.

"There was no doubt in my mind," Danny said. "It was her."

He waited in the lobby, and when the door opened Briana walked out. He said he almost didn't recognize her because she was fully clothed and had dyed her hair super blonde.

"Briana," he said. "It's Danny...."

No recognition.

"We met on Mullholland Drive...."

Instant recall. He said she "went pale." They talked for a few minutes, in low voices, trying not to attract attention. He asked her if she was okay.

"Getting better," she said.

"I heard you scream just now."

She nodded. "Yeah, well, now I've had the practice."

Trying to laugh it off. He told her he was from Massachusetts and she said she was from Minnesota.

"Did you think about going home?" he asked. "Since what happened?"

"Yeah, totally, I almost did," she said. "But then I got a call back, and, you know, I guess I'm still here."

Danny stayed in LA for a few more years. I only stayed another few months, then went home and applied to grad schools. I liked Los Angeles, for the sunshine and the weirdness, but ultimately I couldn't live there. The city didn't have a soul.

Chapter 3

Sertraline Dreams

Patrick arrived at school fifteen minutes late, tired from sleeping through his alarm- again- but energized from the twenty-minute walk. A warm, empty feeling throbbed in his head.

Mechanically he twisted through his locker combination, his brain not yet switched over from Autopilot to Manual. As with many recent mornings, Patrick was thoroughly distracted. Last night, or early this morning, he had dreamed that his closest friends, in cahoots with several more kids he was not very good friends with, in cahoots also with strangers, a few relatives, and random people from his past, had conspired to kidnap Lindsay Burke, for the sole motive, it seemed, of psychologically torturing Patrick.

Patrick took several deep breaths by his locker. He hung up his coat. He collected the books and notebooks for his first two class periods. He closed his locker and just stood there for a long moment. The more urgent matter of coming up with an excuse for being late to Geometry felt like a low boil compared to the spillover anxiety of the kidnapping plot.

It is not real. No one kidnapped Lindsay. Everything is good. You are okay.

He slipped into Geometry with a mumbled apology. Ms. Gennett did not interrupt her demonstration of the proof on the blackboard. Patrick slumped into his desk and quietly opened his notebook.

"Jesus, Pat-Man, who scrambled your eggs this morning?" whispered Jesse from the chair behind him.

Patrick shrugged as Jesse handed him a piece of paper with the current proof on it so Patrick could catch up.

In the dream Jesse had draped an arm over Patrick's shoulders and calmly told him that Lindsay was being held in a barn somewhere, and would stay there until Patrick "stopped acting like such a dick all the time."

"Thanks, man," Patrick said, passing Jesse back the proof.

"Everything okay?"

"Yeah."

Patrick stared at the board, shifted his mind into Manual, tried to focus on the proof. Geometry had become awkward for him since about two weeks earlier when he had experienced a prolonged and graphically sexual dream featuring himself and Ms. Gennett, and one or two other people, including a boy, whose identities were too embarrassing and shocking to contemplate. It was sort of funny, when he told himself it was just a dream. But it was also sort of not funny. The sex dream had felt more like a memory.

"I'm worried that my dreams may be bringing latent sexual deviancies to light," he had told his therapist.

"Everyone has inexplicable sexual dreams," Dr. Caplan replied. "Generally, I believe sexual dreams don't necessarily mean anything. Especially for a seventeen-year-old."

"My dreams have been much more vivid since I started taking Sertraline," Patrick said.

Dr. Caplan just nodded in that quiet therapist way, like anything in the world might be possible, and not a big deal.

Patrick had begun taking anti-depressants four months ago, just after he'd started seeing Dr. Caplan. He did not know if he "suffered from depression," as both his parents and the therapist suggested. All he knew was that over the course of sophomore year, for reasons he could not understand or explain, he felt like he was going to kill himself someday. Someday soon. He envisioned throwing himself in front of the commuter train, which ran near his house. Patrick kept these mysterious suicidal ponderings to himself, and dealt with them by sleeping more and more both at night and during the day, until sleeping was basically all he did, prompting action from his parents.

The initial side effects of the Sertraline had included diarrhea, which had made soccer practice unpleasant for about two weeks, and delayed orgasm, which Patrick had cautiously chosen to consider a sort of blessing. If he ever did get a girlfriend, he would be able to last longer during sex.

But the dreams were unanticipated. They felt like movies, with himself as both director and star. They had complicated and twisting plots, and seemed to last for hours, even by the convoluted standards of dream-time.

"I doubt your dreams actually last hours," was all Dr. Caplan said in the way of reassurance. Patrick's therapist was more concerned about Patrick's constantly thinking about suicide.

The suicidal thoughts subsided, leaving him almost entirely, taking with them, seemingly, a series of other feelings, not all of which were bad, such as caring and sympathy, and sometimes his ability to focus.

Now there were mornings like this one: Patrick sat hunched at his desk, trying to focus on math, trying to laugh at something that wasn't really funny, thinking about both why his friends would want to kidnap Lindsay Burke, and why Ms. Gennett had insisted that Patrick fuck her from behind.

By second period American History he felt a little better, even though in History he sat next to Eric. Eric had been the ring-leader of the kidnapping, smiling his way through a series of disturbingly-specific threats of bodily harm to Lindsay.

"You know why we're doing this, Pat," Eric had told him. "Because you're always such a fucking asshole."

This from his best friend since the second grade.

"You do the reading last night?" Eric asked him in the lull before the teacher began his lecture.

"Most of it," Patrick said, which was true, although he couldn't remember anything. They were studying the Spanish-American War.

"Me neither. Brad said he can get us Adderall before the next test. You want some?"

"God, no."

"You all right, Pat-Man?"

"Just tired."

Eric clapped him on the back. "Tomorrow's Friday."

Patrick nodded. The kidnapping had come to light during an epic weekend party. Everyone was there. Somehow Patrick had known that it was Brad who slipped something into Lindsay's drink so they could abduct her.

Fourth period was English, and Patrick had done the homework. He'd read *For Whom the Bell Tolls* before. It was one of his favorite books. These days he found he looked forward to English, as he looked forward to lots of little things; an unexpected bonus, he assumed, of the drugs.

Except today he watched the door with simmering dread as his classmates filed in and took their seats. The third desk back from the front in the row by the windows was Lindsay Burke's seat. It was empty.

Fourth period was the first of the school day's four lunch periods, so sometimes people were a couple of minutes late for class, having snuck down to the cafeteria for a snack. Lindsay Burke often showed up to class with a coffee, which meant that she had a car, which meant that her movements and whereabouts were potentially in constant flux.

Lindsay Burke did not show up to English. Her desk was the only empty seat. Patrick hunched in his chair and tried to scribble notes, but they were nothing but gibberish. He felt the cold fluttering of nerves in his gut.

It was just a fucking dream. And this is just a fucking coincidence.

After class Patrick could remember nothing about *For Whom the Bell Tolls*. He hurried to his locker to change books and notebooks, hoofed it back across the school and upstairs to the foreign language wing. As he walked his eyes darted through the halls. Other students were smiling and laughing, taking their time at their lockers, lost in a world of infinite leisure and security. A girl smiled at him. Maybe. Maybe it was a tease-smile. Everyone had smiled at Lindsay's kidnapping-party too, even while telling him what a jerk he was.

You're not a jerk.

Lindsay Burke was in Patrick's French class too. That was how they had become friends, stumbling over vowel-heavy pronunciations together, mutually reassured by their shared inability to twist their mouths around the language. French was like English spoken in a dream, sinewy and tentative, meanings uncertain.

Lindsay's desk in French was empty. Mlle. Delong hardly ever took roll-call, and now seemed almost studiously oblivious to Lindsay's absence, pacing the class with her usual composure, her eyes steely and inscrutable.

Patrick responded incorrectly to a verb-tense question, and Lauren Malcolm teasingly looked at him cross-eyed. This made everything worse. He could not focus for the rest of class.

The next period was Patrick's lunch. He stuffed his books in his locker and ran outside to the junior parking lot. Lindsay Burke drove a green Taurus with an old Clinton/Gore bumper sticker left over from when her father had owned the car. She usually parked near her friends' cars by the baseball diamond. Even in the parking lot seats were unofficially saved. Patrick wondered where he would park, if he had a car.

He jogged around the parking lot three times, concluding that Lindsay's car was not there. Could she have parked somewhere else? Unlikely. Juniors got ticketed when they tried to pilfer a Senior or Faculty parking spot.

Glancing up, Patrick saw a kid staring at him out the window of some classroom. He diverted his eyes away from the watcher's gaze and hurried back into the building.

He checked the library, and the cafeteria, and the study corrals, but did not see Lindsay anywhere. He could not remember what class she had after French, or if she had one. There was one way he could probably track her down, but it would take an act of stealth.

There were twelve minutes left in his lunch period. He had not eaten, and wondered vaguely if he should get food. The administrative office was located right next to the cafeteria. He walked through the caf and slipped into the office. He lingered by the empty receptionist's desk as if he needed to ask for a hall pass or an excused absence form. Across the office two administrators were chatting behind the dwarfed ramparts of half-cubicles. Nobody was specifically watching him.

He checked two desks before he found one where the screen saver had not yet activated. The chair radiated human posterior warmth. Quickly Patrick scanned the desktop, clicking through several files until he found the database of student class schedules.

Somewhere a door opened and closed. One of the women across the office laughed.

Patrick hunched forward, staring at Lindsay's schedule. Currently she had sixth period study hall, followed by seventh and eighth period Chemistry plus Chem Lab. Room 414E. Science wing.

Patrick closed the file and snuck away from the desk. He had six minutes left to eat lunch. He ducked out of the office and into the cafeteria, bought a heat-lamp-dried slice of pepperoni pizza and a carton of 1% milk.

About fifteen minutes later Patrick cut gym class and crept up to the Science Wing. He leaned as casually as he could against the door of room 414E, and peeked through the window into the classroom. The desks faced away from him, but he knew most of the kids in the class pretty well, and thought he could pick out Lindsay's brunette ponytail. She was not present.

The evidence pointed pretty conclusively to Lindsay Burke being absent from school. There were only two class periods left in the day. Having skipped gym, Patrick saw no real reason to stick around for Economics, since they were just going to be going over yesterday's test, on which he had earned a pleasantly anonymous low B. He now felt certain that the only way to salvage this weird day, psychologically, was to know exactly where Lindsay was and what she was doing.

Patrick left school and walked briskly down Parker Street toward Minuteman Drive, where Lindsay lived. He had been to her house once before to study for a French test. It was only half a mile from the school. *This is stupid,* he thought. *Crazy and stupid.*

When he reached her house he saw her green Taurus parked in the driveway. That was good. Probably. Maybe she was home sick. Or maybe not. There were no other cars at the house. He walked up to the front door and rang the bell.

Nobody answered, so he rang again. Knocked. Nothing. It would be stupid to give up now. He still had to walk all the way home, and he knew if he didn't find her he would not be able to concentrate for the rest of the day.

Around the back of the house Patrick climbed the wooden steps to the porch. Through the sliding glass doors he could see the living room and part of the kitchen. There were no lights on. No television. He leaned against the glass for a better look, knocked firmly with his knuckles.

Tentatively he tried pulling the door, and it slid open. His stomach tightened.

You should not be doing this.

He took a step into the house.

"Lyndsay?"

For a moment he stood in the living room, listening. Then he closed the porch door behind him. "Lyndsay? It's Pat."

He walked from room to room, clutching the straps of his backpack, ears tuned for movement or voices. The house smelled of recently-vacuumed carpet and something canine.

You should get out of here.

His feet made no sound on the carpeted stairs to the second floor. He stopped on the landing, glanced left and right. Took a step left and peered into what looked like the master bedroom. He felt a weird, warm stirring in his gut.

"Lyndsay?"

He turned around and walked down the hallway to her room. The door was open a crack and he pushed it wide, revealing the perfumed chamber within. Lyndsay's room was clean and relatively neat for a high school girl. There were stacks of books and DVDs on the floor by her television. Her wall was covered with photos of her friends. There was no clothing anywhere.

Patrick went into her room and sat down on her bed. He set his backpack on the floor. He wanted to cry. This did not look like the bedroom of a girl who had disappeared under nefarious circumstances. It just seemed like she wasn't home. And what the hell was he doing in her room? He felt so tired, not just in his body but in his mind. His eye sockets tingled, and his sinus burned, the way they did when he felt an anxiety attack coming on.

Just get yourself together and then go home, he told himself as he lay down on the bed.

He was walking down Parker Street again, kicking orange leaves, watching the foliage in the trees.

What the hell? Didn't I just do this?

He felt no sensation of the cold air. Passing cars made oceanic whooshing sounds.

Oh, shit, I'm asleep.

But the details of Parker Street were crystal clear. He knew that he had been at school that day, and he remembered the dream about Lyndsay being kidnapped, and he remembered walking to her house. But he wasn't at the house yet. And Parker Street seemed unusually long.

He felt the panther before he saw it, knew instinctively somehow that it was stalking him through the neighborhood. Rounding the corner onto Minuteman Drive, he saw the enormous cat slinking along in the bushes.

.Shit!

Now he was on the roof, and it was his own roof. Lyndsay Burke's house was nowhere in sight. And it was summer. Patrick crouched on the edge of the roof and peered across the lawn at the toolshed in Mr. Griswold's yard. Somehow he knew that if he reached the toolshed he would be safe. There were weapons there. The panther watched him from a neighboring roof, its tail flickering a warning.

Patrick jumped off the roof and sprinted for the shed. The cat sprang off its roof, running toward him, then running behind him, then it leapt and knocked him to the ground. Its jaws bore downward, tearing out his throat-

He sat up on Lyndsay's bed, his heart pounding. He knew somehow that he had heard a door close. He climbed off the bed.

What the fuck am I doing here?

"Pat?"

Patrick stood stark still, staring at Lyndsay in her bedroom doorway.

"Oh my god, Lyndsay."

She was half-smiling, surprised but not alarmed. "What's up...?"

No excuse immediately came to mind, and one of the positive things Patrick had learned through therapy was that telling the truth always trumped lies, evasions, or misdirection. Telling the truth purged the soul.

"This is going to sound fuckin' nuts," Patrick said. "But last night I had this dream...."

He told her the details, how her absence from school had ultimately led him here, how he was happy to see her, and sorry for intruding into her room. He told her even more, about his therapist and the Sertraline, how the drugs made him feel generally better, except at night, when all his buried worries and fears seemed to come clawing after him.

"I think I'm going crazy," he said.

Lyndsay took a tentative step into the room. "I went to look at colleges with my mom today. That's why I wasn't in school."

She walked over to him, saw that he was shaking. "So how much was the ransom?" she asked.

They both sort of laughed.

"My sister was on anti-depressants for a while," she said. "She did some wacky shit. Sometimes it takes a while to get the dosage right."

"I know I shouldn't be here," Patrick said. "I'm just so glad you're okay."

He thought he might cry, and she put a hand on his arm. "I'm okay," she whispered. "Everything's okay."

"Lyndsay?" Lyndsay's mom called from down the hall. "Who are you talking to?"

"Pat's here."

"Who?" Lyndsay's mom appeared in the doorway, arms crossed and regarding Patrick with a look somewhere between scrutiny and suspicion.

"Patrick, from my French class," Lyndsay said. "He just came by to give me the homework I missed today. He saw my car in the driveway."

"Actually, no," Patrick said to Lyndsay's mother. "I just had a bit of a freak-out. I had this weird dream last night, and woke up thinking that something bad had happened to Lyndsay. I guess I had to prove to myself that she was okay."

"Everything okay now?" asked Lyndsay's mother.

"Yeah, we're good," Lyndsay said.

"You guys aren't in some kind of trouble, are you?"

Patrick vigorously shook his head.

"It was just one of those weird things," Lyndsay said.

"Patrick, honey, you look like you're still half-asleep," said Lyndsay's mom. "Would you like some coffee, or something?"

"Thank you," Patrick said. "I would."

Walking home he felt energized from the coffee. He and Lyndsay and Lyndsay's mom had sat at the kitchen table drinking hazelnut roast and telling war stories from the trenches of prescription drugs. Then Lyndsay had offered him a ride home. He had refused. Needed to clear his head, he told them. Get some fresh air.

The November air did feel good, cool and cleansing as he breathed it in. He was still trying to laugh about all this. It would be funny, he thought, if it was happening to somebody else.

On the way home Patrick crossed the railroad tracks, and he glanced up at them with genuine ambivalence. He no longer really thought about jumping in front of a train, and when he did, it was only to wonder what had made him think of doing that in the first place.

When he came to his own street it was almost dark. He had slept most of the afternoon in Lyndsay's bedroom. Something moved on the roof of his neighbor's house and he stopped, the hair on his arms suddenly tingling.

There was nothing on the roof. It might have been a squirrel. Or a bird. Or a cat. But nothing now.

It is not a fucking panther.

But the street felt as real as it had in the dream. Patrick turned a full circle, reassuring himself that his neighborhood was not being haunted by an animal that was not even remotely indigenous to this area. And yet he felt like he was being watched.

He ran the last few hundred yards to his house.

There is no fucking panther, everything's okay. There is no fucking panther, everything's okay.

There is no fucking panther. Everything's okay.

Chapter 4

A Dark North Territory

Jasper, Maine – 1878

There was not a sound in the world. The snow-covered pine trees stood deathly still beneath a tombstone sky. Joseph Tracker stood outside his cabin, inhaled a deep, icy breath. The storm had dumped a foot of fresh snow on the hard February ground, and more was on the way.

The village of Jasper was a mile south. Joseph could smell fires burning in the houses of town, but he was not headed in that direction. He was going north, to the Mallets' cabin, an onerous trek in winter. He supposed Harrison and Sarah had survived the storm. Harrison was proud of his ability to carve a habitation out of territory so desolate God himself had no interest in it. But Joseph worried about

Sarah. She was a city woman, cultured, unaccustomed to backwoods survival.

And she had left him the note.

He had built his cabin on the edge of town three years ago, after Martha passed, as a refuge from the settled life that had betrayed him. Out in the wilderness he lived unsettled, with the raccoons and bears and fisher martins- none of whom made their presence known today. All creatures seemed wise enough to hunker down.

Joseph stepped into his woodshop to gather supplies. First he found his French calfskin knapsack, left to him by his brother Richard- now deceased- after the War Between the States. Inside the pack he placed a buck knife, twenty feet of good rope, his tinderbox, a hatchet, a pound of smoked venison jerky wrapped in cheesecloth, a pound of chopped potatoes from his winter store, a cookpot, a canteen for water. He attached his canvas tent and woolen bedroll to the knapsack. From the wall he took down the snow shoes he had made himself. Wearing them he could travel twice as fast, and they prevented him from plunging into holes where his leg might become encased in snow. Frost bite had taken his uncle Roger during the winter of '56- not a fate Joseph hoped to meet. Joseph had recently made a second pair of snow shoes, for feet slightly smaller than his own, and these he strapped to the knapsack as well.

Before leaving the shop he scrawled a note bearing his intentions, to be left on his work bench in case anyone came calling. Reading and writing were still shaky new to him. With much concentration he was able to pen a terse message: "Gonn to Mallets cabbin to see if alive. Hard snows coming. Left Toosdaye." The words did not all look right, but they would have to suffice. Joseph stepped outside and closed the door to his workshop. He wrapped his woolen coat around his neck, and trudged into the snowy labyrinth of trees.

The soft crunch of his snow shoes barely penetrated the silence of the forest. The air was too cold for a thaw. Tendrils of snow hung from tree branches. Joseph followed the frozen white band of the river north and west. With no sun overhead, and no shadows to measure time, he could only estimate his progress. There was no point guessing the miles anyway. He would hike until he reached the Mallets' cabin.

In town folks speculated that this was the worst winter since '56, when the post office roof caved in. Uncle Roger had met his end tracking an escaped cow across his farm. Tripped in a hole and sunk to his waist, froze to death staring at the trickle of smoke from his own chimney. This winter the snows had buried Jasper. Joseph trekked to town whenever he needed supplies, or to remind pesky Reverend Wilkes that he was still alive. But mostly he was content to ride out the winter in the solitude of his workshop, building furniture for sale come spring, and practicing the letters Sarah Mallet had taught him.

The trek to the Mallets' cabin and back would take him probably two or three days, depending on the weather. Joseph thought it unlikely that anyone would come looking for him while he was gone. His only real concern was Reverend Wilkes. The pastor had recently escalated his effort to rope Joseph back into the herd. Since Martha's passing Joseph had attended Church sparsely, and that more for the human company than the sermons. Martha had been the Reverend's passionate disciple, attending First Baptist since she was a child. It was Wilkes who had married them, Wilkes who had ardently implored them to start producing children for God. Martha had obeyed; within months of the marriage their first child was brewing. But her blood came early. Reverend Wilkes arrived to pray for the mother and unborn child, but both were lost, their shared lifeblood pooled out like a lake beside the hearth. Joseph had held his wife in his arms as she died.

"We do not question God's will," Reverend Wilkes proclaimed in ostensible sympathy. "We only trust He is fulfilled, with these two beautiful souls beside Him in His kingdom."

Joseph was not consoled by this speculation. He knew his wife had been virtuous on their wedding night. She had bled then too, which he took as a sign that her womb was not yet ready for new life. Better they should practice at it, he had thought. He had enjoyed the feeling of his wife, and though he knew his duty to God, he had wanted time with Martha alone. They could enjoy each other on frigid Maine nights, the sweet scent of burning firewood curled in their nostrils, their warm skin pressed together.

But at the Reverend's urging Martha had wanted a child, and Joseph blamed their haste- the Reverend's haste- for the termination of his family.

Sarah Mallet had moved to Jasper to become schoolteacher, the long overdue replacement for old Hattie Phelps, taken three years prior by the consumption. She came from Boston, was educated in letters, mathematics, history, geography, and the Scriptures. Joseph knew her from First Baptist. She was polite and thoughtful, mannered in a way that bespoke the city, a clear outsider in the earthy hamlet of Jasper, but with a quiet dignity he respected.

Her incongruous choice of mate was baffling. Harrison Mallet was dirty and boorish, a trapper by trade, and a lout, illiterate and scornful of the printed word, renowned in Jasper for his explosive temper and his ignominious habit of toting around his kills. Rare was the occasion when Harrison was seen in public without the corpse of a beaver, a coon, or a fox slung over his shoulder, the blood and rot of his kill-stained clothes producing a smell few would liken to honeyed biscuits.

The Mallets' marriage had produced a daughter who had perished in infancy. After the baby's death Harrison had moved himself and his wife out to the cabin in the woods, beyond the tentacle reach of the nosy Reverend, and in isolation the Mallets had lived on since.

The need for a sturdy wooden washboard had brought Sarah trekking through the woods in search of Joseph, the only man in Jasper whose own isolation earned Harrison's stingy trust. Joseph was not opposed to taking payment in trade, but when he glimpsed Sarah's shame-faced offering of a blood-stained raccoon pelt, he informed her that he already had one just like it, and it served him well as a bed pillow. Sarah smiled and requested a bill of sale for the washboard, to which Joseph sheepishly admitted he could not produce one. "No such ability," he said. Sarah perked up at his confession, and a deal was borne. Once a month, on her supply runs to town, she would stop by Joseph's cabin and instruct him in letters, as payment for the washboard.

The lessons became the highlight of Joseph's month. He made tea and scones, and together they retired to the workshop, where Sarah instructed him using the Bible, the only book he owned. Joseph watched eagerly as she emerged from her quiet shell to teach him. When she departed he spent the next month studying, writing out long passages, and re-writing them, sounding out words to get them right. Each month when she returned he opened the Bible to their last marking place and tried to impress her with a recitation of its passages. Rarely did his effort fail to produce a smile. But Joseph was not oblivious to Sarah's true comportment. Often he glimpsed through peeks in her clothes the bruises on her skin. On occasion she caught him noticing her wounds, and she turned away. It was a husband's right to correct his wife if occasion demanded, but Joseph had never condoned such practice. When fall turned to winter, the lessons ceased, and he did not see Sarah again once the first snow fell. But he continued to study his Bible, and in turning the pages he came across a message written in her patrician scrawl, one last assignment, or perhaps a plea:

"Mr. Tracker, I will not survive a winter in isolation. If our lessons have taught me anything, it is that you are a good man. Please find a reason to visit our cabin. Do not let me perish in such dark territory. S Mallet."

Joseph crouched by the frozen river, pulled his hatchet from his pack. He cleared a patch of snow and hammered through the ice. Clear water bubbled from the hole. He dunked his canteen beneath the surface, filled, brought the spout to his lips. The streamwater rushed down his throat.

Watchful of the sky, Joseph trekked until dusk, but did not reach the cabin. He stopped by the river beneath a thick wedge of trees, contemplating his options. He could soldier on, following the stream through innumerable miles in the dark. Or he could hunker down, pitch his tent, build a fire, complete the journey next morning. The sky answered for him, opening in the gloaming to release a swirling downpour of snow.

Joseph pitched his tent by the river. He hacked down tree branches and set them in a pile. Carved a shallow hearth and built a thin fire, adding smoky pine boughs. He ate some jerky, warmed himself with tea boiled in the cookpot. He knew the small store of branches would not be enough to last the night, so he spent an hour in the dark chopping wood until he had built up a decent pile. Finally he slipped into the tent, pulled on his extra clothes, crawled into his bedroll. With his head only a few feet from the fire, he achieved a modicum of shivering warmth.

Joseph revived the smoldering ashes of his fire before dawn, boiled some potatoes for breakfast, washed them down with hot tea. He knocked three inches of snow off his tent before breaking it down.

The forest was a white-washed mystery, blinding bright in the morning sun, silent as the deepest cavern of Hell. Joseph's footsteps made no sound as he followed the stream. He hiked for a long time before he finally caught the scent of burning wood. The trees were thick and impenetrable, and he did not see the cabin until he looked up suddenly and nearly ran into it. His heart beat faster as he imagined Sarah's proximity. He indulged the fantasy that she would be glad to see him as he knocked upon the door.

The door swung open and Joseph found himself staring down the barrel of a Winchester.

"Mallet," Joseph whispered, his throat parched from the cold.

"That you, Tracker?" Harrison Mallet growled.

"It ain't Lincoln's ghost."

The Mallets' cabin contained two rooms, a front room with hearth and counter space, a second room for sleeping and storage. The Mallets only owned two chairs, so Joseph sat on the floor against the wall, happily sipping hot coffee and venison stew brought to him by Sarah. She had indeed smiled when she saw him, an encouraging reward. Harrison grumbled curt misgivings, calling Joseph a fool for hiking out to them when snow still threatened to fall, but the gruff man did not seem entirely displeased by Joseph's arrival.

"Figured I'd check on you," Joseph said.

"Well, you came a long way for nothing."

"Not for nothing, Harry," Sarah said quietly. "Mr. Tracker journeyed to confirm our well-being."

"You can tell the Reverend we're still kicking. With or without his Church."

"It's admirable you've survived this long, Mallet. But don't you think you both would be safer in town?"

"The herd bleats at stray sheep," said Mallet. "Soon as a town gets a Church it loses the essence of the land. We're pioneers, my wife and I. We live on the fringe. That's what Maine is."

Sarah stared at the floor.

"Tracker, it is a good thing you're here," Harrison said. "Last night's gale brought a pine down on my ice house. Reckon with two sets of arms we could get it off."

"Happy to oblige," Joseph said.

After the coffee and stew Joseph and Harrison set out into the cold. Both men looked up to see that the blue sky of morning was being steadily usurped by thick clouds.

They trudged through knee-deep snow to the ice house, where Harrison kept his kills. A trunk of pine a foot thick lay across the ice house roof. Splinters of wood and shingles littered the ground. Harrison slapped his meaty hand on the trunk. "Should've taken her down in summer," he said. "You learn hard lessons out here."

"Why learn 'em?" Joseph asked, pressing on the trunk to test its weight.

"I never slept well on lace pillows." Harrison pointed to the roof of the ice house. "Reckon if one of us climbs up, pushes from there, one stands here and does the same, we'll have it off."

It took them several heaves to liberate the trunk from the roof. Finally on their fourth or fifth sweat-breaking push the fallen tree floated to the ground, lodging itself deep in the snow. Standing on the roof, Harrison stared at the gaping wound in his ice house, a jagged gash where snow and rain could now pour in. "Well, carpenter, I don't suppose you brought us a hundred shingles in your pack?"

"Not even one," Joseph replied.

"I can thatch it with pine boughs till spring," Harrison said. "I'm handy with an ax and saw."

He indicated the cabin. Joseph stared at the log concoction, the smoke dribbling out of the chimney. He thought of Sarah inside, confined to those two rooms, her lonely mind starving for books and company.

"A weak man leans on the comforts of town," Harrison said, climbing down off the roof.

"You've done well," Joseph conceded.

Above them the last of the blue sky vanished.

"Tastes like snow," Harrison said.

Back in the cabin, Joseph leaned against the wall next to his knapsack, his snow shoes resting beside him.

Harrison checked the barrel of his Winchester and pulled on a thick pair of wool socks. "It's time to hop to," he said. "I've got to check my traps, and Tracker's got many miles back to the lace pillows."

"Perhaps none of us should venture out," Sarah said. "If another storm is imminent."

"If my traps are buried, we'll lose a dozen kills," Harrison said.

"Better to dig a few holes for traps tomorrow than to dig one for us tonight," Sarah remarked.

"Stores are low," Harrison said. "You'll be cooking your books and eating all them fancy words if I lose my traps. And Tracker will want to be on his way in advance of the storm."

"A dangerous prospect," said Sarah.

"We've seen worse and will again," said her husband.

Sarah glanced at Joseph, concern in her eyes. "I really think none of us ought to leave."

Harrison strode forward and grasped her throat. "Sarah, I've no qualms correcting you before a guest. Tracker was married once, he knows my right. I've set my mind, and it shall be so."

Sarah flinched, but did not turn away.

Joseph saw his opportunity. The bull-headed man was going with or without their approval. "Mrs. Mallet, I believe your husband's in the right. In this territory the smart man tends his resources."

"Maine ain't no place to hope the next meal will just come along," Harrison said.

"Perhaps I could remain briefly while Mr. Mallet checks his traps," Joseph suggested. "Gather my strength and supplies, and depart upon his return."

"It don't take four hands to throw another log on the fire," Harrison said. "But I'll use you for insurance, Tracker." He reached into a drawer in the kitchen table and pulled out an hour-glass filled with white sand. "The storm might come on fast. If I'm not back in two turns, do me the favor of lacing up your snow shoes. I see you brought two pair just in case."

Joseph watched as Sarah's eyes flicked toward the extra snow shoes.

"Start north and west, come 'round in a circle," Harrison said. "You'll see my trail. I don't expect any winter sprinkle to get me after all these years, but it don't hurt to be safe."

"Two turns," Joseph agreed, setting the hour-glass upside-down.

"More stew when I return," Harrison said on his way out the door.

They passed the first hour with a lesson. Sarah read passages aloud from her Bible, and Joseph copied them in his scratchy hand, using a charcoal pencil on old birch paper.

"Your progress is notable, Mr. Tracker," Sarah said as she observed his letters.

"I'm grateful for your lessons, Mrs. Mallet," Joseph replied.

Together they watched the last few grains of sand drain from the hour-glass. With a perfunctory glance at Joseph, Sarah stood and turned the glass over. Joseph noticed that she sat down with uneasy swiftness, her hands fidgeting as she glanced into the smoldering hearth.

"Mr. Mallet knows the forest," Joseph said. "I've no doubt of his safe return."

"Nor I," said Sarah. "Mr. Mallet always reaches his destination, no matter how foolish the journey."

"Mrs. Mallet, does this cabin suit you?"

Sarah considered the question. "Mr. Mallet and I have indeed chosen a unique patch of ground to call home."

"I wonder if you might prefer living closer to town. This stretch does not seem ideal for a family."

"Maine is a hard place for a family," Sarah said.

In each of their lives there was a ghost child. Joseph had glimpsed his infant only long enough to discern its sex- a girl- before Reverend Wilkes had whisked the lifeless gray pod away, sparing Joseph and Martha the sight of their expired offspring as the life-blood drained from Joseph's wife.

"As I have said previously, Mrs. Mallet, I am sorry for the loss of your daughter."

Sarah forced a smile. "As I am for yours, Mr. Tracker."

Joseph felt his chest tighten. Remembering his little girl, whose eyes never opened once in this world, he thought of his own remote abode, and how suffocating the loneliness of civilization's edge could be.

They remained quiet for a long time. The cabin was stiflingly small, and growing colder as the fire died down to embers. Finally Joseph stood up and retrieved a log from the pile beside the hearth. "May I?" he inquired.

"Please," Sarah said.

Joseph added two more thick hunks of wood, and the fire rejuvenated, yellow flames licking up the chimney.

"Mrs. Mallet, I don't mean to tread upon your burden," Joseph said. "But how did your daughter come to pass?"

Sarah stared at him uneasily, her mouth a tight frown.

"I ask merely as a concerned neighbor," Joseph elaborated. "For it seems she was born, then passed, then you and Mr. Mallet immediately quit Jasper. I too respect the desire for privacy, as you can see from my remove."

"The cause of death was not... natural," Sarah whispered.

"An accident?"

"I do not believe there was any malice intended," Sarah said carefully. "But poor Emily was colicky. And Mr. Mallet's nerves are... delicate." She said the word forcefully, as if it were a curse. "She was screaming, and I was unable to stop her. I cradled her and sang to her, but the colic persisted. Mr. Mallet seized her–"

Joseph felt his chest tighten with rage.

"–and covered her mouth with his hand." Sarah wiped at fresh tears. "I tried to take her back, but he would not allow it and... eventually the screaming stopped."

Sarah looked up at Joseph again, her angry eyes burning red. "My husband is a brute," she said. "I did not see it at first. I thought he was rugged and unspoiled, a man of action and capability. I was lonely and new to town when we married. I knew no one and I trusted the Reverend. Foolish girl. And now I am his prisoner, confined in this wooden cell."

Joseph glanced at the hour-glass, watched as the last few grains of the second turn tumbled home.

Sarah noticed too. She and Joseph exchanged a glance, in which there was no urgency, but a strange mote of understanding. Together they continued watching, for a length of time neither could determine.

"I had expected the door to swing open by now," Joseph said eventually.

Sarah nodded. "It has been two turns. He was likely delayed untangling some squirming *thing* from one of his traps."

They remained seated, unmoving. Eventually Sarah stood. "I will start a fresh pot of stew. Mr. Mallet will be hungry when he returns."

"The light is dying," Joseph said. "And the storm is not breaking."

"My husband is a resourceful woodsman," Sarah said. She picked up the hour-glass. "But I think the risk of venturing out is not equal to the reward."

"You know him better than I, Mrs. Mallet. I defer to your judgment."

"We'll compromise," Sarah said, turning the hour-glass, and setting it once again upon the table. "I shall prepare a fresh pot of stew. We both shall keep a vigilant eye on the storm, and we will give Mr. Mallet one more turn of the glass."

For the next hour they made a pretense of readiness. Joseph paced by the door, his coat drawn over his shoulders, the snow shoes resting against the wall. Sarah filled the kettle with chunks of meat and dried vegetables, set the pot over the fire to heat. They spoke little. Sarah made tea and poured each of them a cup. They sat at the table and sipped in silence, watching the sand in the hour-glass dribble away.

When the glass was nearly empty Sarah retrieved the stew from the hearth. "Well, Mr. Tracker," she said. "If you need to search for Mr. Mallet in darkness, you should fill your belly first."

"Thank you," Joseph said.

Together they ate a slow meal. Joseph savored the tender, meaty stew. Rarely did he cook for himself with any flare beyond venison jerky and canned fruit.

They acknowledged the new emptiness of the hour-glass with a short, mutual glance, turning back to their meal as if the time piece was not important.

When he finished eating Joseph stood and opened the door. Outside snow swirled in thick gusts. The forest was pitch black.

Sarah stood in the doorway beside him, squinting into the storm.

"It will be slow going," Joseph said.

"Mr. Tracker, I see no benefit from your leaving this house," Sarah said. "Furthermore, I fear that if the storm claims both my husband and yourself, I will likely perish alone at this cabin from lack of resources. That's three lives cost for the price of Mr. Mallet's obstinacy."

"I hoped conditions would improve," Joseph said. "But they have not."

Sarah took a long, deep breath. "I admire your courage, sir, but I must insist that you remain here."

Joseph closed the door, his chest flooded with relief. He was not a fool. A hundred paces into the woods and he could become hopelessly lost. His faith in Harrison Mallet's survival at this point was minimal. Nevertheless, he returned to the table and flipped the hour-glass once again. "Mrs. Mallet, I feel assured that by the fourth turn either your husband will arrive, or the storm will let up."

"Let us pray on both accounts," Sarah said.

They passed another hour by the fire. Sarah inquired about various members of First Baptist. Joseph supplied information where he could. But his remove from the church, and his disinclination toward Reverend Wilkes, shortened his responses. Eventually the hour glass once again drained empty in a thin cascade of sand.

"There is nothing more to do," Sarah said. "The storm is God's will. I think we must wait for morning."

"That's my instinct as well," Joseph said. "Were Mr. Mallet in our place I'm sure he'd mark the danger."

"Let us take a hard lesson from my husband's pride," Sarah said. "Mr. Tracker, the hour is late. I'm afraid our accommodations are scant, but you are welcome to make use of this room."

"I have adequate supplies," Joseph said.

"We shall reconvene tomorrow, then. Good night."

"Good night, Mrs. Mallet."

Sarah walked into her darkened bedroom. There was no partition or door, just an empty entranceway. Joseph unpacked his bedroll and positioned it near the hearth.

The fire crackled to a low hiss. As he drifted off to sleep he expected to hear muffled sobs, or perhaps a prayer for her husband's safety, but instead all he heard was Sarah's measured breathing, as if she were deeply relaxed and at peace.

By morning the storm had cleared, and the sky was a piercing blue. Joseph stood outside the Mallets' cabin, marveling at the heavens. The Maine sky was a moody mistress, blustery one moment and serene the next, defying one to accuse her of any foul temper.

Joseph heard the rustling of branches, the distant sounds of animal life. The February air was still cold enough to steal one's breath. He wrapped a scarf around his face, and set off into the woods, heading north and west, per Harrison Mallet's instructions.

He made nearly an entire circle before he found the body. It leaned against a tree, sitting cross-legged, a pool of frozen blood encircling an oddly-bent leg. The skin on Harrison's face was gray-blue, like frozen lakewater. His beard was a white mask of snow. His mouth hung slightly open, as if his dying breath had been a gasp.

Joseph crouched beside the body and placed a hand on its shoulder. Harrison's mouth twitched. Joseph fell backward in surprise.

"Mallet?"

"Tracker...." His voice was nearly gone.

"Good god," Joseph said. "What happened?"

He handed Mallet his canteen, and the other man drank. Blood and spittle dangled from his lip.

"I stepped... in my own trap...." With a frozen hand he pointed to his foot. "Had to... hack it off...."

Joseph stared at the injured appendage and took in the grim details of the scene. A bloody buck knife protruded from Mallet's belt. After performing the savage operation, Mallet had apparently pulled his boot on over the stump. A trail of bloody footprints wound back into the forest. Joseph wondered that the man had not bled or frozen to death. Likely the cold had stopped the bleeding.

Harrison Mallet breathed in short, aggravated bursts. He glared at Joseph. "It's been more than two turns of the damn glass," he hissed.

Joseph nodded, thinking of the distance to the cabin. From there it was a long trek to town. And the man had severed his own foot.

"I'll help you," Joseph said, and he stepped forward to lift Mallet off the ground.

Mallet draped a strong arm around Joseph's shoulders, and they set off into the woods. It was a slow and excruciating trek, Mallet wincing and crying out in pain with every step. Joseph took frequent breaks, guiding them steadily uphill. Above them the blue sky drained away like water being poured from a pan, replaced by thick gray clouds. Joseph could taste the coming snow.

"Let me down!" Mallet eventually cried, clenching Joseph's shoulder.

Joseph leaned the man carefully against a stump. "Let me lighten your burden," he said, removing the Winchester from its perch on Harrison's pack. Joseph stepped backward and sat on the trunk of a fallen tree.

"I know perfectly well what you're doing, Tracker," Mallet growled.

"Meaning what?"

"The cabin is in the other damn direction."

Joseph stared at him silently, checked the rifle to see a cartridge in the barrel.

"I know this land like I know my own mind," Mallet said. "You're leading me off."

"It's your land," Joseph said. "I'm following you. Helping you back to the cabin. Perhaps in your injured state you are confused and lost."

Mallet nodded, his breaths now coming even shorter, his limbs weighing him down like sacks of dirt.

"She ain't what you think she is," Mallet said. "I know what you think she is, and she ain't that."

Joseph said nothing, thinking of how long it would take him to trek back to the cabin.

"She's the one killed that baby," Mallet said. "Covered its mouth with her own hand."

"You're lying," Joseph said. "She told me otherwise."

Mallet looked up at him with pain in his eyes. And something else. Sadness. It was not a look of prevarication.

"She done it before," Mallet whispered. "Told me she done it in Boston too. That's why she come up to Maine. Nobody looking for her in the dark territory."

Joseph fingered the trigger of the gun. One shot and it would all be over. But then what story would he tell in town? If he just waited for death to come naturally, Mallet would be buried in snow, no fault but his own.

Joseph lay down the rifle and walked over to Mallet. Crouching in the snow, he took hold of the boot on Mallet's injured leg.

"Tracker-"

Mallet screamed as Joseph pulled the boot off, revealing the frozen purple stump of Mallet's ankle, the sliver of exposed bone encrusted in blood. Joseph took the boot and slapped it down against the wound. Mallet wailed and fell backwards into the snow, his stump pouring fresh blood.

"You ain't no doctor," Joseph mumbled. "That's a poor amputation."

He stood and followed his footsteps back down the hill, leaving Mallet to holler in pain. Soon the cries died out, and fresh snow began to fall.

Returning to the cabin, Joseph found Sarah sitting by the fire.

"Did you find him?" she asked.

"He's gone. Stepped in his own trap."

Joseph watched as the news seemed to glance off her like a puff of wind. Her lips nearly curled in a smile, but she seemed to catch herself, lowering her head and pressing her hands against her skirts. "A predictable outcome," she said quietly. Her eyes flashed to the pair of snow shoes Joseph had brought with him, leaning against the cabin wall. "Mr. Tracker, I do not wish to remain at this cabin a moment longer. I'd be grateful if you'd guide me back to town. Perhaps to your own lodging?"

Joseph still held Harrison's rifle, and he gripped its trigger guard as he leaned against the wall.

"He was alive when I reached him," Joseph said.

Sarah's look faltered momentarily. Joseph watched as she composed herself to reflect concern. "You saw him expire?" she asked.

"We spoke first."

She stared at him patiently.

"He said you killed the baby."

Sarah's mouth straightened into a frown. Joseph saw a steely resolve in her eyes he'd not seen before, certainly not in the seeming innocence of their reading lessons. "That's not the truth," she said.

"He said you done it before. That's why you came to Maine. Which is no place for a city girl."

Sarah's expression hardened again. There were no tears in her eyes, and no trace of remorse. "Harrison Mallet was an angel compared to my first husband," she said. "I have only known mean men. And I will not raise the devil's spawn."

Joseph gripped the rifle. Sarah took a step forward.

"You're kind, Joseph," she said. "There's no devil in you."

Joseph reached down and picked the snow shoes off the floor. He shouldered the rifle and put on his pack.

"I'm no different or better," he said, and he turned and walked out of the cabin, leaving Sarah to the snows, and the winds, and the whimsies of God.

Chapter 5

Coyotes

Piercing screams ripped Enid Thorne from sleep. She grabbed the shotgun from beneath her bed, bounded downstairs in flannel pajamas and a pink tank top, charged out the front door. Found Kaylie crying in the driveway, cradling the bloody carcass of her cat.

Enid saw the culprit slinking away across the field, the mangy brown coyote, head and ears low to the ground. She ran ten steps, aimed, fired a deafening blast that socked her skinny shoulder bone. The coyote dodged into the woods.

Heart pounding, Enid lowered the gun. Kaylie stared up at her, covering her ears. Janice, Enid's mother, stood in the doorway, holding a steaming cup of coffee up to her face.

"Mommy?" Kaylie asked, her fingers bloody from the eviscerated cat.

"I'll get him next time," Enid muttered. She safetied the shotgun, bent down and touched her daughter's shoulder. "Poor little kitty."

"He isn't afraid to come right into the yard," Janice said, taking a long sip of coffee. "I'd've got him myself, but I wasn't up yet."

Enid glared across the field toward the green line of the woods, where the animal had disappeared into territory he knew better than she did. She was not afraid either, not of predators that crossed the line onto her farm.

The farm sprawled over a hundred and twenty acres on the outskirts of Walter's Walk, population 438, a village buried so deep in Western Maine that Rand McNally had either failed or neglected to pinpoint it on the map. Enid had always felt that her hometown was on the road to nowhere. Walter's Walk sat thirty miles from the Canadian border. The barren stretch of Maine mountains felt like a foreign country. She had seen a city only once in her life, Boston. She had seen plenty of Portland when her father was dying in the hospital, but Portland was hardly a city. The farm, and the lone strip of decrepit houses in the Walter's Walk village, were all the America she had ever known.

The farm had belonged to her father, who had barely produced enough livestock and crops to sustain. Henry Thorne had tilled the land for thirty-five years on the slow descent to bankruptcy.

Enid now managed what was left of the farm. At night she worked as a cashier at Laverdier's Grocery, twenty miles away in Jackman. Her mother listlessly saw to various tasks around the barn, milking, feeding, corn-husking, while keeping an eye on Kaylie. During the summer the two women managed to produce and can enough food to save money on groceries. Come winter Janice too went to work at Laverdier's, in the mornings, so that she could truck back to Walter's Walk to pick up Kaylie from school while Enid worked the night shift.

Two things had driven Enid Thorne to the sobriety she needed to run the farm: the birth of her daughter, and the death of her father. Before sobriety her life had been a tornado. With nothing for a young woman to do in Walter's Walk except drink, drug, and fuck, Enid had stormed through her teen years with her eyes closed and the loaded gun of addiction pressed against her head. Then the little blue line had fizzled up on the home pregnancy test she'd stolen from Laverdier's.

Rich chocolate soil marked the grave of Kaylie's cat. Kaylie patted down the pebbly dirt with a trowel, while Enid and Janice observed a silent vigil. Enid wanted to bend down and wrap the girl in her arms- Kaylie was the love of her life- but she held back. This was a hard moment, and she wanted her daughter to appreciate the finality of death, to understand the gravity of the forces at work against them. The world sometimes brought random and uncountered violence. Later that night, when they were cuddled in bed, Enid could assure Kaylie that they would find her another pet, but for the moment the Maine earth had called back one of its scions.

"That does it," said Janice, who was given to statements of the obvious, particularly since Henry's passing. Her husband had always responded to her commentary with agreement. In the three years since his death from colon cancer Janice had gradually emerged from the glum fog of grief to an attitude of acceptance.

On their way back to the farm house, Enid heard the low rumble of a pick-up truck. She instinctively stepped in front of her daughter.

The pick-up wheeled to a dusty halt in front of the house. For a moment nobody got out of the cab. Kaylie reached for her mother's hand.

Both truck doors opened at once and three men stepped out of the cab as casually as if they owned the place. Jeremy, Orton and the Dumb One lined themselves up and folded their arms almost in unison, a single creature with three heads. Enid glared from one of them to the next, wishing she had her shotgun.

Dipshit Jeremy stared curiously at Kaylie, the way he always did. Enid knew what he was thinking. There was a good chance that Kaylie was his daughter, although the little girl might just as likely have come from Orton. Orton stared at Enid with dead porcine eyes, his fat face locked up in a perpetual frown. The triumvirate was rounded out by the muscular man who leered at all women with lupine hunger. Though Enid referred to him as the Dumb One, his real name was Rick, and she was smart enough to know that he was not just some dumb animal. Rick was Orton's half-brother, and he was dangerous, as were his two companions, both of which Enid had known intimately, much to her regret.

"Did you all just come out here to make our day worse?" Janice asked, standing a safe distance from the men. "Or do you have something to say? We can't read your minds."

"It would be a short story if we could," Enid grumbled.

"We were just out back rounding up a batch," Jeremy said, jerking his thumb toward the woods. "We have a new arrangement for you."

Orton grunted, and Enid felt her stomach tighten. Jeremy leaned slightly forward and grinned at Kaylie, his mouth short several teeth. "Hey there, baby," he said.

Kaylie waved at him, stared at the ground without speaking.

"So what is it?" Enid asked, angry that she had allowed the men to glimpse her daughter.

"We're gonna build a lab out in them woods," Orton said. He had the tinny voice of a child, and Enid shuddered when she heard it.

"What are you talking about?" she asked.

"Meth lab," Jeremy said, turning his joker's grin on her.

"A what-now?" Janice asked.

"I don't agree to that," Enid said.

"Don't matter," Orton said. "We'll show you the spot when we pick it out. It'll be underground. We'll be digging at night."

"You've got your acre for pot, that's all I'm willing to give up," Enid said.

"Don't matter," Orton repeated.

"Everybody's growing pot," Jeremy said. "Market's saturated. Meth's the new pay-dirt."

Orton turned back to the truck, signaling the end of the pow-wow.

"We'll be back soon," the Dumb One said, standing in the driveway a moment longer than the others.

"Can't wait," Enid spat, although she could not meet the demented, dancing look in his eyes. She suffered the Dumb One's presence with caution, never forgetting what nasty things he would gleefully perpetrate upon her if he ever caught her alone.

The men climbed back into the truck and rumbled away down the road. Jeremy waved to them out the passenger-side window. Enid flipped him off.

Fuckhead Jeremy had been Enid's first crush. She had known him all her life. He had been the first boy in their class to own a ten-speed bike, the first one to shoot a deer with his father's rifle, the first to find older kids to buy them beer and pot. With his dark good looks and easy charm Jeremy had seemed to Enid like the only boy in town with any chance of getting her out of Walter's Walk, so she had glued herself to him. The ride he took her on spiraled from marijuana and alcohol to mushrooms, cocaine, and OxyContin, and all the while Jeremy never left his parents' basement. He still lived there, when he wasn't slinking around town with John Orton and his pack of vermin.

Fuckhead Jeremy had screwed Enid out of a future with his laughing empty promises that selling drugs would earn them enough money to live the life they wanted. She had allowed him to screw her whenever he wanted, starting when they were thirteen. She would cling to the awkward thrusts of his pale body, hoping to prevent his eye from finding someone else. When the drugs had taken hold, she had allowed him to screw her in other ways, screw her out of money, let his conniving cohorts screw her when they wanted to. Jeremy possibly screwed her up finally and completely when he or one of those other assholes had planted their seed in her. The seed had grown into a baby that Enid was too broke and scared to abort, but which she'd sworn to herself she would hate and torture for all of its miserable life, to get back at the men who had fucked her. The baby had come screaming into the world on the kitchen floor of the family farmhouse, with only Janice for a midwife, and had looked up at Enid, bawling as if to say "I never asked for this either," and Enid had instantly fallen in love.

It had been Jeremy who had swooped in to save the day when Enid and Janice were facing foreclosure on the farm. John Orton would pay them a little something to cover the bills, in exchange for an acre of land in the vast unmonitored woods of the Thornes' property, an acre on which he could grow whatever he pleased. The deal was cash for silence, and Enid had accepted. Selling a piece of her birthright in sobriety stung worse than any of the times she sold a part of herself in the drug-addled fog. But it was either that or face homelessness. She had a daughter to think about. And her mother. Janice didn't like the arrangement either, but Enid's mother knew there were forces in life beyond your control.

Enid met Holly for after-work drinks at The Roundtable, Walter's Walk's only bar. The squat gray building with the broken sign contained neither a round table nor any patrons who could ever be confused for knights. Holly, once overweight but now a gaunt, yellow thing, sucked down Jack and Cokes, while Enid quietly stirred a cherry in her glass of ginger ale.

"Fucking Jeremy's got himself a little whore in Jackman," Holly complained. "Know how I know? I stole his cell phone and dialed every fucking number."

Enid stared at her friend's gray gums and rotting teeth, and wondered how in blue fuck the two of them had ever mutated from little girls riding horses at Holly's farm into this: twenty-six-year-old specters haunting the only bar around for miles, no longer bothering to imagine what life might offer them beyond Walter's Walk. They might have been eighty years old, or dead, it didn't matter- Enid knew their chance to escape had long passed. She did not even care that Holly was now shacking up with Jeremy, had been for two or three years. It was a shallow dating pool. But she was disturbed to see how far down the pipe Holly had followed him. Holly sat across the table exuding a terrible smell. Whether it was her breath, clothes, cigarettes, or life in general, Enid could not tell.

"You should leave him," Enid said. "Clean yourself up. Come on out to our place and work the farm for a few months. It'll do you good."

"I've seen too much corn and canned apples," Holly said. She drew on a thin cigarette, her fingers twitching like the wings of a fly.

"You can't go on like this," Enid said. She thought of her daughter, wanted to return home, curl up in bed with her kid. Holly always called with some disaster she wanted to hash out.

"Things aren't so bad," Holly said. "We'll be making money soon, when Orton gets his lab up and running. I tried to talk them out of building on your land, but Orton and Jeremy both said it was best. You can keep your mouth shut. Guess we owe you one."

Enid's blood boiled. How did her friend already know about the meth lab? She could feel the eyes of the mischievous men in the bar turn upon her. Maybe everyone knew what was going down on her farm. She glared right back at them. Nobody would stand up for her. Half the folks in town bought pot and God knows what else from John Orton. The men at The Roundtable gazed at her with winks and grins, dogs waiting patiently for the cat to let down her guard.

"Nobody's building a lab on my land," Enid huffed, grabbing her purse to leave.

"Wait," Holly said, downing the last of her Jack in one shaky gulp. "I need a ride."

Enid floored her old station wagon down the rumbling country roads, her eyes burning in her head.

"Where are you going?" Holly asked. "We passed my road."

Enid screeched to a halt in the dirt driveway of a crumbling wood-frame house hidden deep in the woods. Lights of various colors leaked out of the house, illuminating the dark pine trees. Trucks parked at odd angles in the driveway.

Holly sat up straight and looked around nervously.

"You shouldn't be here," she said.

Enid ignored her and turned off her car. Stepped out into the night and trotted up to the house. Rapped on the withered front door, loudly.

The door peeled opened. She expected to see Orton standing there, but instead the Dumb One loomed over her, grinning like he'd been waiting for her. A bottle of whiskey dangled from his hand. The butt of a pistol peeked above the waistband of his jeans. Beyond him in the smoky house she could see other men, heard Orton squealing up some scheme.

Enid faced up to the Dumb One. He was a full head taller than her. "Tell Orton I reject his proposal," she said.

The Dumb One nodded, took a contemplative sip of whiskey, then snatched out a hand and grabbed her shirt. "Get your cute cunt in here and tell him yourself."

Enid tried to pull away, but his grip was too strong. Suddenly Holly appeared beside her, shoving the Dumb One back inside the doorway. "Don't touch her, Rick."

The Dumb One turned his wolfish grin on Holly. "Holly, you look just about right."

Holly grabbed Enid and pulled her back toward the car. "Come on, kid, we're going."

Enid looked back over her shoulder at the Dumb One, clutching her car keys with a shaky hand. "Tell your brother what I said," she told him as Holly steered her away from the house.

The next day she drove to Jackman with Kaylie to buy feed for the pigs, and when she returned to the farm she could tell something was wrong. A chicken fluttered in the ditch beside the driveway. She hopped out of the car and grabbed it, set it down clucking in the back seat.

She found Janice standing in the yard, hands on her hips, shaking her head. The barn door had been smashed open. Enid ran to her mother, yelling back at Kaylie to stay put.

"What the fuck happened?" Enid said.

"Just got home," her mother said. "I was playing bridge with the girls. It's pandemonium."

Chickens bounced and fluttered across the yard. Their cow was nowhere in sight. Someone had driven through several rows of corn, trampling a healthy swath of crop.

Suddenly Enid heard the panicked squeal of a pig. Looking across the pasture, she saw the mangy coyote chasing the pig into a corner of the stone wall. The wild dog sunk its teeth deep into the pig's hide, and Enid saw a spurt of blood shoot from the rump of her hog.

"Watch Kaylie." She sprinted into the house, took the stairs three at a time, dove under the bed for her shotgun. Her father had kept an old twin-barrel in the barn for general protection against wilderness invaders, but Enid had purchased her own weapon for defense of the home, a Mossberg 500 Flex Tactical, 12 gauge, 6-shot pump. She ran across the field toward the dying pig and stopped only when the coyote looked up at her. She fired at him just as he leapt the stone wall, once again evading her shot.

Enid collapsed to her knees, sucking in deep breaths, her chest burning, tears in her eyes. "Fuck you!" she cried at the coyote, at the forest, at goddamned Jeremy and John Orton and everyone else in shithole Walter's Walk.

She did not lament long. The dying cries of the pig rang in her ears. She stood up and walked over to it. It thrashed in the corner of the field, its eyes filled with panic and confusion, blood gushing from deep bite wounds. Enid wiped her eyes, whispered a few words of respect, and shot the pig in the head.

When Kaylie was safely abed, Enid sat in the kitchen with her mother, the two of them splitting a kettle of chamomile tea.

"We can't call the sheriff," Enid told her mother again. She lowered her eyes to avoid her mother's disapproving glare. "The deputy is John Orton's cousin, Jesse."

"Is this my property, or not?" Janice grumbled, and Enid could not argue. "I won't see your father's farm disgraced or vandalized by dope-growers. I want to call the sheriff and explain everything. It's still my damn property."

"We can't pay for it, Ma," Enid said. "And if the cops find the weed, they'll seize the farm. It's our land, we're responsible."

"I don't like being bullied."

"Neither do I. We just need to stand our ground. If it's a fight Orton wants, he'll get one."

Janice snorted, shaking her head over her tea. "Listen to you, little girl. Where did you come from, I've wondered more than once?" She pointed to the ceiling, toward Kaylie's bedroom. "You're going to wage war with dope-growers? I don't think so."

Enid knew her mother was right. Her tough-talking only made her feel childish. She could never risk her daughter's safety. Not with Walter's Walk crawling with coyotes.

"I wish we'd never lived here, Ma," Enid muttered. "I wish Daddy had moved us to Belfast and farmed lobsters instead of corn."

"One place is as good as another," Janice said, her non-teacup-holding hand clenched in a fist. "It's the drugs that are ruining everything."

Enid stared down at her small, pale hands. They were shaking, and smelled of gun powder and pig's blood. She closed her eyes and took a deep breath. After a moment her pounding heart rate settled to a softer beat and her hands sat perfectly still.

For two days the farm was quiet. It was late-August. The corn was rounded at the ends of the ears, ripe for picking. Enid, Janice, and Kaylie spent long hours in the field, harvesting for trade in town. They wrapped fresh ears in tin foil and grilled them for supper.

Holly called Enid in one of her usual panics, said she needed to meet at The Roundtable. Enid said she could only spare an hour. She drove into town just before dark, the setting sun like a blood orange dribbling toward the horizon.

The Roundtable was virtually deserted.

"Jeremy's off fucking his Jackman whore," Holly muttered, already drunk.

The promised hour turned into two. Enid's ginger ale tasted cheap and syrupy.

"Come on, kid," she told Holly around eleven o'clock. "I gotta get home."

Holly seemed even more nervous and fidgety than usual, but she sprang to her feet at the prospect of a ride.

They cruised away from The Roundtable and headed deep into the woods, to Holly's trailer. Enid saw a truck sitting in the driveway.

"Who's truck is that?"

"'S'mine," Holly slurred, stumbling from the car before Enid could stop her, or make her recant the lie.

Enid watched her friend trip in the driveway and fall to her knees. Not at all in the mood to play babysitter, she stalked from the car, leaving the engine running, and grabbed Holly beneath the armpits.

"Get up." Enid was strong for a small girl, but Holly did not make it easy. Plus she was crying now, and apologizing, a familiar routine that Enid did not want to hear. When they reached the front door Enid was not at all surprised to find it unlocked. She pushed it open and shoved Holly inside. Reached for the light.

A cold, sharp crack took her in the back of the head. She pitched forward into darkness.

Face pressed into Holly's cheap, turd-colored carpeting, Enid's eyes crept open. The trailer was dimly lit from a shadeless low-watt lamp, and she could make out the legs of a table, crumbs and candy wrappers on the floor. A pair of men's boots. The boots moved, and she heard a hiss of laughter. Holly was nowhere in sight.

Her head throbbed with pain, and for some reason her ass hurt too, and she realized her jeans were at her knees. Curled in the fetal position, she groped for her pants, staring up through bleary eyes at the ghoulish face of the Dumb One.

"Don't worry," The Dumb One said, buckling his belt. "I used the back door. Don't want another little bastard running around, do ya?"

"Fuck you," Enid croaked.

"Just did." The Dumb One laughed, then he was on the floor on top of her, his knee driving into her spine. "You're gonna go on home tonight and clean up. You'll see what I mean when you get there. And you're gonna keep fuckin' quiet. Starting tomorrow we're digging that lab out in them woods." He drove his knee further into her back. Pain rippled through her entire body. "You just shut your mouth, and this will work out good for all of us. You'll see."

An eternity later Enid peeled herself off the floor of Holly's trailer, and staggered outside to her car. It was still running, the high beams blaring into the forest. The pickup truck was gone. Tears poured down Enid's face. How could she have let her guard down? How could she not have sensed a trap?

She sat in the car for a long time, sucking back tears, allowing her eyes to focus on the night forest. Then she remembered what the Dumb One had said about cleaning up a mess, and she swung the car out of Holly's driveway and floored it home.

This time they had left the barn intact. No animals were loose in the yard. They had trashed the house. The screen door had been ripped clean off, and the old front door gaped open, a gash of torn splinters. Enid ran inside. Janice lay slumped against the wall, eyes closed, mouth drooling open, holding ice wrapped in a dish towel to her head.

"Mom!"

Enid fell to the floor beside her mother, stirring Janice awake. "That you?" her mother groaned. "Oh, God, baby, they took her. They took Kaylie."

There was blood on Janice's face, and a sizable purple lump on her skull, but Enid registered none of this. Icy sweat bristled from every pore. She ran from room to room, screaming her daughter's name, moving so quickly she barely felt her feet touch the floor. She checked the basement, the closets, under the girl's bed. Her daughter was gone.

She ran to her bedroom and grabbed the Mossberg, wrenched a box of shells out of the closet. She loaded up in the living room, headed for the door.

The phone rang.

It was three o'clock in the morning. Enid snatched the receiver and hissed into it before the caller could identify himself. "Touch her and you'll die slowly," she promised.

"Easy, mama bear."

Fuckhead Jeremy. Of course. Orton would never place the call personally, never implicate himself.

"Here's how it's gonna go down," Jeremy said. "I've got Kaylie over at my place. She's fine. She's asleep right now. Quiet little angel-"

"Jeremy, I'll be there in ten minutes-"

"Shut your mouth, Enid! Listen to me, or I swear to God, bad things will happen. You listen to me now."

Enid said nothing, just gripped the phone, breathing fire.

"Kaylie's gonna camp out with me for three, four days," Jeremy said. "We're gonna send some guys in to dig that lab. Lay the concrete, install ventilation, get the generator up and running. It'll run on gas, so there'll be no power lines, nothing to make anyone suspicious. Once we're done, we'll bring Kaylie home, and everything will go back to the way it was."

"You bring her home right now, Jeremy, or we'll go to the cops."

"You mean Sheriff Jesse?" Jeremy snickered. "I see a State Trooper's car coming down the driveway, Enid, I'll shoot the girl."

"You wouldn't."

"All you have to do is shut your mouth and this will all be over."

Enid said nothing.

"She's mine too, you know," Jeremy added, sounding almost hurt.

"She's not yours," Enid countered. "Even if she's yours she's not yours."

"She's got your eyes, looks like, but that's my father's chin."

"Jeremy, listen to this." She put the phone down, racked her shotgun so he could hear the cold, metallic slide, then slammed the phone into the receiver.

Enid cried until just before sunrise, leaning against the wall next to her mother, clutching the shotgun. Janice wafted in and out of consciousness, her words coming in bursts and slurs. Twice her hand went limp and she dropped the dish towel full of ice. Enid stood up and helped her mother to the car. She buckled Janice into the passenger seat and drove to the hospital, half an hour away.

At the emergency room she told the doctors they'd been in a car accident, and both she and her mother were treated for their injuries. Enid did not mention the throbbing pain in her rectum. When she checked herself in the pungent, urine-smelling hospital bathroom, she saw a smear of dried blood in her underwear. She cried silently for several minutes, then pulled herself together and rejoined her mother.

Janice's X-rays confirmed a concussion, with internal bleeding under her skull. She was admitted, and Enid rested in the bed beside her all the next day.

At dusk her mother came to. Enid sat beside the bed, holding her hand. "They took her," Janice whispered. "Said if we called the cops they'd kill her."

Enid nodded, four Percocets deep and feeling little pain.

"The doctors need to monitor you for a few days," she told Janice. "There's still a lot of swelling. As long as you're here, you'll be safe. Just lay low and get better, and don't talk to anyone. Don't call the police. I'm going to get Kaylie back, and fix everything. I'm sorry I was a pain in the ass all those years, Mom. Look where it got us."

"Enid, honey," Janice said, tears brimming in her eyes. "Please don't lose your head."

Trees snapped like bones beneath the claw of the backhoe. Night by night the diggers unearthed a cavernous black mouth in the forest. They poured thick concrete into the hole, carved out a square room, lugged their equipment into the bunker. Slapped on a concrete ceiling, punched ventilation holes, filled the earth back in. Built a plywood shed to house the generator. Chiseled out an entry shaft and tacked on a manhole cover.

Enid watched the entire construction from the shadows of the trees, hiding just beyond the yellow fingers of the floodlights. Like a ghost she haunted the worksite, listening to Orton's guys joking and cursing, watching the machines and trucks rumble through the thick woods. The men had no idea they were being watched. Enid sat for hours, perfectly still, watching every move with the patience of a mountain cat. She learned the woods like a wild, feral thing, memorizing every tree, every ridge, every boulder. She did not sleep. She listened to the animals, the calls of the birds, felt the gentle wind in the trees. Mosquitoes bit her until she bled. She wiped her blood on scratchy tree trunks. She became the dark territory she did not know.

During one long night's watch the coyote stumbled upon her, stopped to stare at her. She turned calmly and his moonlit eyes met hers.

"You're next," she whispered.

When the meth lab was nearly complete, the men dragged barrels of gasoline out into the woods to power the generator, set them up in a row beside the shed, covered them with a green tarp. Enid smiled. The fucking idiots had carted their own demise right out to her.

Mumbled conversations arrested as Enid filled the doorway of The Roundtable. Behind her the setting sun slipped out of sight behind the trees, wanting no part in whatever she had planned.

Holly looked up from her Jack and Coke, eyes wide, knee shaking like a jackhammer. Enid wanted to grab her by the hair and smash her face through the table. Kick her teeth in and punch her eyes shut. Instead she walked quietly over to her friend. The old whiskery rodents at the bar turned away. She stood inches from Holly's face, pulled out a pack of cigarettes.

"Come outside for a smoke," Enid said.

In the car Holly started blubbering. "I had no idea, E, no idea they were gonna take her. I swear they used me, just like they're using you."

"No one's using me," Enid said, glaring through the twilight at the road. "I'm using you."

When they reached Holly's trailer Enid parked her car around back, out of sight. She led Holly into the house, through the unlocked door, into the filth-strewn living room. Sat her down on the couch. Reached into Holly's purse and handed the frightened girl her cell phone.

"Call," Enid said. She placed a sheet of handwritten notes on the coffee table, brushing aside a moldy pizza box. "Say it right, or you go to prison for kidnapping."

Holly swallowed hard and spoke into the phone. "Rick? Hey.... Yeah, not much, man, just sitting here alone, thinking about things.... What kind of things?" She glanced at Enid. Enid pointed to the paper. "You know what kind of things," Holly said. "Jeremy's been fucking some whore out in Jackman.... Yeah, I know you know, everybody knows."

She read Enid's scratchy, demented handwriting. "Come on over here and help me get a little payback."

The Dumb One arrived half an hour later, swaggering out of his truck, adjusting his John Deere baseball cap. Enid watched from the window, her eyes narrowed. She had retrieved the Mossberg from the car, and now she turned it on Holly, who stood next to the couch, shivering naked beneath a thin blanket.

"Drop it," Enid ordered. "Make sure he sees you. Pose if you want."

Holly dropped the blanket and leaned against her La-Z-Boy, her naked body tainted by stretch marks and repulsive sores from God knows what. Enid looked away.

The door to Holly's trailer squeaked open and the Dumb One sauntered in, grinning as he saw Holly preening for him.

"That's about right," he said.

Enid stepped out from behind the tobacco-stained curtains and planted the stock of the Mossberg into the back of the Dumb One's knee. He winced and fell to the ground. He turned to face his attacker with murder in his eyes, but Enid racked the pump of the gun.

"Lie down," she commanded, and the Dumb One complied, sweat budding on his brow. Enid tossed Holly a length of bailing twine. "Tie his hands to his belt, then get dressed."

Holly hurried over to the Dumb One, wrapped the splintery twine around his wrists. Enid noticed there was a tear in the seat of the Dumb One's pants, through which she could see a patch of yellow-stained underwear. She stuck the barrel of the Mossberg into the tear.

"Keep quiet," she said. "Or I'll use the back door."

The bus station in Jackman was deserted when Enid dropped Holly off. Neither of them knew when the next bus was due, probably not till morning. Holly stood shaking on the sidewalk, her thin possessions crammed into an old Sea Dogs duffle bag. Tears trickled down her cheeks as she counted the small stack of cash in her hands.

"I swear I didn't know," she said. "I'm sorry, E."

Enid nodded, wishing she hadn't given Holly two hundred and fifty dollars, nearly her entire savings, but she wanted to make sure her old ex-friend stayed gone.

"What am I supposed to do in Boston?" Holly asked. "I don't know anyone there."

"Get clean," Enid said with a shrug. "Get a job. I don't care. If you ever come back to Walter's Walk I'll dope you up and make it look like an accident. No one will question it. Everyone in town knows you're a junkie."

The words burned in Enid's mouth. Who was she to pass judgment? Were it not for a broken condom she would likely be exactly where Holly was tonight, minus the wad of cash. She could not look her friend in the eye. Holly wiped her face, took out her cigarettes, lit one.

"Aw, fuck it, kid," she said, exhaling a cloud of purple smoke. "I always wanted to leave this shithole anyway."

Enid nodded and drove away. It was many miles back to Walter's Walk, and she wanted to get back to the woods, where the Dumb One was tied up, before the coyotes robbed her of the satisfaction of devouring him.

John Orton's squealing voice answered on the third ring. "I told you never to call this number," he spat in lieu of a greeting.

"I don't care," Enid said. She stood in the woods, straining to maximize the lone bar of reception on her phone. "I'm at your lab. With your brother."

The Dumb One was tied to one of the ventilation pipes sticking out from the upturned soil. Duct tape secured the rag stuffed in his mouth. He reeked of the gasoline Enid had poured over him.

"What's that dumb shit doin' over there now?" Orton hissed. "We ain't startin' till tomorrow night."

"He's atoning for his sins," Enid said. "And so will you. Bring me my daughter right now, and I'll let him go."

"Let him go? Who the fuck are you?"

Enid kicked the Dumb One in his injured kneecap, and he released a long groan of pain. "You won't have much of a brother left, if you don't hurry," she said.

She crouched in the shadows, invisible. The Dumb One squirmed against the ventilation pipe. The moon rose high above them like a spectral eye. Enid smoked cigarettes and waited for the men. They arrived an hour later, parking at the end of the dirt access road that snaked through her property. They tromped through the woods with flashlights. Enid could hear Kaylie complaining that it was dark and she was scared, and her heart quickened.

Enid had been busy. Using a hose and a bicycle pump she had siphoned almost an entire drum of gasoline out into the forest, spreading an intricate web of combustible fluid over the dry ground-cover. She had doused trees and shrubs, criss-crossed a thousand square-foot area around the lab, encircled the site with an invisible perimeter of gas. She had left a small ten-foot section of forest unscathed, an escape route that only she could locate. The trap set, she had gone into town to ambush Holly and the Dumb One. Her clothes reeked of earth and sweat and gasoline. She smoked in blatant defiance of the fumes, a human furnace, breathing fire.

The men wandered obliviously into her circle of death. John Orton kneeled over his brother and began to question him. The Dumb One could not speak with the gag in his mouth. Orton pulled out the gag.

Jeremy held Kaylie in his arms. The girl did not appear overly distressed, just tired and dirty. Enid stepped out of the shadows behind her ex-boyfriend and swiftly snatched her daughter. Jeremy, Orton and the other men turned, angry, to behold the earth-ridden mother bear clutching her cub.

"Enid?" Jeremy squawked.

"What the fuck do you think you're doing?" John Orton squealed, his pig eyes black in the night.

Enid ignored him, kissing Kaylie and stroking her hair. Kaylie squeezed Enid's neck, buried her face in her mother's shoulder, noticed the cigarette sticking out between Enid's lips.

"Mommy, smoking is stinky," Kaylie said.

"You're right, baby," Enid said. She pinched the cigarette in her fingers.

The Dumb One wrestled free of his restraints and staggered up off the ground. "Kill that fuckin' bitch," he growled.

Orton, Jeremy and the others reached for the guns in their belts. Enid flicked her cigarette at the Dumb One. The big man ignited like a torch, flooding the forest with light, screaming as his flesh cooked beneath his fiery clothes. Orton and the others turned in confused circles as the entire forest erupted around them. Enid clutched Kaylie and vanished into the trees.

Blinded by fire and smoke, the men screamed and fired their guns. Enid pressed Kaylie into the earth, shielding her from the shots. The remaining gas tanks at the meth lab exploded as Enid knew they would, and the vast swath of Maine woods that had been her peaceful property moments ago burned like the eternal caverns of Hell.

Enid tucked Kaylie into a small hole she had dug that morning. She removed the Mossberg from its hiding place beneath a pine branch, crouched by the gap in the wall of fire and waited.

"Mommy, I'm scared," Kaylie cried, coughing from the thick smoke.

"I know, baby," Enid said. "We just have to make sure all the bad men are gone."

The dope growers could burn for all Enid cared. They deserved to be incinerated for the rapes and murders they had committed, upon her, upon her land, upon their town. But she suspected that Jeremy the Worm would somehow slither out of the trap. Like he always did.

Sure enough her ex-boyfriend emerged a few minutes later, staggering through the woods, singed and black, clutching a pistol and coughing into his shirtsleeve. He saw Enid glaring at him and stopped, his red eyes full of pain and panic and maybe a little wonder.

"Cover your ears, angel," Enid said, and Kaylie dutifully obeyed her mother.

Enid raised the Mossberg and shot Jeremy once in the chest. Jeremy slumped backward, fell first onto his ass, then back against the forest ground, his body quickly engulfed in flames.

Enid grabbed Kaylie and ran back to the farm.

The lies rolled off Enid's tongue like smoke rings. No, she was not aware that a gang of marijuana dealers was using her land to grow their product. No, she had no idea that they had been building a meth lab in her woods. No, she did not know they had installed a gas generator, a malfunction of which had apparently caused the fire that consumed more than fifty acres of her family's property. She was the victim of malfeasance. She had awoken to screams and gunshots in the night, stumbled into the woods with her shotgun to investigate, saw the terrible flames devouring the forest. She had not recognized Jeremy as he staggered out of the fire, had shot him in self-defense when she saw the pistol in his hand. She was devastated over the destruction of her property, shaken to the bone for having killed her ex-boyfriend.

The State Police believed everything. Sheriff's Deputy Jesse Orton glared at her as she spilled her guts, biting his lip until it bled. She knew he would not contradict her, would never tell the Staties about all the times he had turned a blind eye to John. Holly would not come forward either; she was tucked away in Boston with two hundred and fifty dollars and a fear of Enid's wrath. Janice, laid up in the hospital, knew nothing about the fire, and followed Enid's careful coaching on the issue of John Orton and the meth lab. Kaylie was never questioned.

Enid returned to the farm with her mother and daughter. Together the three of them rebuilt their fences and fortified their barn. They replanted their corn. Enid allowed a contractor to haul away the burnt trees on her property, sold the detritus for compost and fertilizer. Together they lived out the summer under the fearful eyes of Walter's Walk.

No one approached Enid Thorne with accusations or questions. No one dared approach her at all.

In early September Enid found the mutilated corpse of another unlucky barn cat. Kaylie had a new pet now, a house cat named Boggs, and Janice had adopted a German shepherd puppy from the animal rescue in Skowhegan. But the feral spree-killer still stalked the farm, rising from the ashes of the forest.

Enid snuck out at night and sat in the tall grass of the cow pasture. She poured a thermos of coffee and loaded the Mossberg. Sat perfectly still in the damp field, eyes trained on the woods. Overhead stars drifted lazily across the sky, and just as the moon ducked behind the trees, quietly renouncing any part in Enid's plan, the coyote slunk out of the woods.

It trotted toward the barn, head and ears low to the ground, eyes sharp and alert. It stopped ten feet from Enid, noticing her too late. She took careful aim at the stunned intruder, exhaled a breath of hot, demonic air, and blew the coyote's brains out the back of its head.

Chapter 6

Effigy

The antique shop had a fire escape along the back wall facing the mill stream, and every kid in Clayton knew that the third-floor window was never locked. Moira Johnson and a few of the seventh-grade girls claimed to have snuck into the shop a few times, and we believed them, because they smoked cigarettes.

On a summer day when we were about eleven and were supposed to be riding bikes around town, Jess Castellano, Alecia Farmer and I pedaled up to the antique shop and hid our bikes behind the ghostly white building. Lecie peeled her pink foam helmet away from her sweaty hair and stashed it beneath the spokes of her front wheel. Jess and I did not wear helmets.

The antique shop was only open on weekends, when old Mrs. Helstrom emerged from her cat colony on Cedar Street to conduct business. I had been in there a few times with my mother. It was like three creaky floors of somebody's storage closet, filled with the kinds of things you put in the attic. Old clothes and doll houses and picture frames.

Moira Johnson had stolen a 1920s-era woman's hat from the antique shop. The hat smelled of mold, and came from who knows where to get to Clayton, Maine, population 1,470. I did not care about hats. I wanted to see the Book.

The fire escape's closest step was about three feet off the ground. Jess gave me a boost, and I pulled her up behind me. Lecie stayed behind, standing next to her bicycle.

"I don't know, guys," she said, frowning up at us. "I don't want to get in trouble."

Little Lecie the baby. I had known she would chicken out. Jess and I only invited her along so we could watch her squeal.

"Stand watch then," I said. "Whistle if anyone comes along."

Jess and I left Little Lecie twisting her hands beside the mill stream. Gripping the rusted railing of the fire escape, we climbed to the third floor.

I peered through the window into the black cavern of trunks and boxes, my heart nearly in my mouth. Jess leaned in beside me. I could smell the flowery detergent scent of her tee shirt.

We pushed the window open and climbed inside. The stale air was choking thick. The floorboards squirmed beneath our feet.

"Where is it?" Jess asked.

"On the second floor."

She stopped and touched my arm. "What is that sound?"

I froze.

Tentacles of violin music rose up through the floor from somewhere in the lower unknown.

"Someone's here," Jess said.

"No. It's Wednesday."

Sweat dripped down my sides from my armpits, pooled beneath my eyes, beaded on my lips. If I had been alone I probably would have turned back, but Jess was with me, and I had promised her we'd find the Book.

"I think someone left a record player on," I whispered.

The music grew louder as we tip-toed down the musty stairwell to the second floor. My imagined bravery evaporated by the moment. We inched into the main display room of the store. It was empty. There was a record player, spinning out Vivaldi. Jess stared at the music machine and pinched my arm.

"Mrs. Helstrom's ghost," she whispered.

I laughed, terrified.

Together we crossed the room to a display case and peered down through the misty glass. The Book was leather-bound and three inches thick, like a dictionary. The cover showed two sets of bare legs intertwined below the tantalizing title: *The Big Book of Sex.*

"Told you," I said.

We crept around the counter and liberated the Book, lifting it out of its case and setting it on the counter. Jess traced her finger along the embossed letters of the title. "Emma," she said. "You first."

I peeled open the Book to a random page. The Book was illustrated, in graphic detail. The image we happened upon was a bedroom scene like none I had ever imagined. At eleven I knew almost nothing about sex, just that I wanted to know more. The picture showed a naked woman bending over a naked man, who was sitting on a bed with his legs spread, his penis long and thick and pointing straight up.

The woman was placing some sort of ring around the penis, like some perverted wedding ceremony.

Beside me Jess took a deep, shuddering breath. The warm skin of her arm brushed against mine, and my chest seized with a feeling like panic, only it was hot, and I liked it.

We turned the pages, absorbed more seedy images into our fertile minds. There was a man holding his penis inches from the inviting, leg-spread vagina of a smiling woman. There was a man and woman twisted like a pretzel in some weird shape that reminded me of snakes, their faces between each other's legs, no bed or anything to give context, just an act being performed in space. We kept turning and found a picture of three naked people sitting on a couch: a woman, legs open to reveal what seemed like an extremely hairy vagina, sat between two men, and in each of her hands she held one of their penises.

Suddenly I felt scared. There was so much I did not know. Was this kind of thing actually done?

"Look how big they are," Jess said, and her finger brushed the creamy paper where one of the penises stood erect.

Without even thinking I reached down and touched the page over the other penis, and together we burst out laughing, sweating, leaning into each other. Then we seemed to understand that perhaps the sneak had gone far enough, and we shut the Book and dropped it rather gruffly back onto its shelf beneath the counter. We had accrued enough stolen knowledge to make us legendary at school, and now it was time to go.

We sprinted upstairs to the window.

My hands felt like Jell-O as they gripped the railing of the fire escape. I descended carefully, worried I might trip and fall. Jess said nothing as she hurried down behind me. We jumped to the ground. There was no sign of Lecie.

"She's such a chicken," I muttered. Something had changed already, and I felt unreproachfully superior to Alecia Farmer, our scared friend who had stayed behind. I was even scornful of her for leaving.

Then I heard her voice.

Jess and I picked up our bikes and hurried out from behind the antique shop. There was Lecie, standing with her bike about thirty feet away, eyes downcast, two adults looming over her.

"Oh no," Jess whispered.

It was Mrs. Helstrom and her son, Michael. She must have been in the shop, and left for a moment. That's why the music was playing.

Lecie was crying. When she looked up and saw us, she pointed in our direction, and I felt tears welling up behind my eyes too. We had not stolen anything, not like Moira Johnson, but how would we explain the Book?

The adults started walking toward us. Jess stood beside me, her arm touching mine again, only this time it was clammy and cold.

"We're in trouble," she said.

My cell phone rang as I was driving home from dropping Kelsey and Ryan off at soccer practice. I groped for the button of the hands-free on my steering wheel, pressed it and introduced a hollow gasp of static into the car. "Hello?"

"Emma?"

"Yeah."

"Hey."

"Hi. Sorry, who is it? I'm on the hands-free."

"It's Jessica."

She pronounced it Yessica, with a Spanish inflection, the way we used to do when we were kids.

"*Hola*, Yessica."

Brief pleasantries. I spoke to Jess only two or three times a year these days, so a call from her always revved up my little girl engine, but I could sense that she was trying not to sound overtly chipper.

"You checked Facebook lately?" she asked eventually.

"Not on much anymore."

"Oh. Well. Alecia Farmer died. Two days ago."

In the movie version of my life that often played in my head alongside the real, unfiltered version, the Emma character might have pulled over to the side of the road to absorb this news. But in twenty-five years life had thrown me its share of punches, and I had hardened accordingly. I was on my second husband, my first set of kids, had a soul-sucking job and a Subaru Forrester. I'd lost my mother to cancer, my favorite cousin Annie to a car accident, and an ex-roommate to suicide. I hadn't seen much of Alecia Farmer in the recent reels.

"I'm sorry to hear that," I said. "Were you in touch with her?"

"Not much, no."

I passed the Dunkin Donuts where the cops always hung out, saw the cruiser crouching in the parking lot, felt as usual like it was waiting there specifically for me.

Jess told me about the funeral, said it was this weekend and she planned to attend. She had always felt sorry for Lecie, never knew what drove her from being such a shy, timid kid to the grown-up train-wreck derailing through

Clayton. I told Jess I would consider the funeral, and eventually we hung up.

November was a hard month to drive home in. It was already dark when I pulled into the driveway, not yet five o'clock. I sat in the car for a while and thought about Alecia Farmer. Her death could hurt me if I wanted it to, if I let it. And a part of me wanted to square off and let the hurt throw a few punches. But the light was on in the living room. Derek was home and I had dinner-prep duty before my aerobics class. There was no time to wallow. I stared at my husband's Prius and wanted to crash it full speed into a rocky abutment, watch as hungry flames engulfed it. A funeral pyre to our suburban self-righteousness. There were days when I just plain did not like myself.

In the living room Derek sat hunched over his laptop in front of the television, checking his fantasy football stats. He held up a hand in greeting, but did not look at me.

"I chopped all the veggies already," he said.

If he had not said this I might have skipped my evening homecoming kiss, but I actually felt a little better as I bent forward and pressed my head against his.

"Are you beating Dave Lewis?" I asked.

"Barely. How was school?"

"They said it was fine."

"You're off and running?"

"I am."

"We just need to marinate the pork chops. I'll help you in a sec."

I peeled off my jacket and dropped it on the couch.

"We might need to have Sue take the kids to soccer this Saturday," I said, staring into the darkness of the kitchen.

Derek looked up from his laptop. "Why? What's up?"

"We're going to a funeral."

We met Jessica and her husband, Chad, for coffee before the funeral at Millie's, one of two restaurants on the gray Main Street of Clayton. It was a two-hour drive out to Clayton. Since my mother died and my father moved down to Portland to be near us I had hardly been back to my hometown. Behind Millie's, visible through the rear windows, was the antique shop, long closed.

Jess and Chad each gave me a long hug, and I remembered, as I usually did when I saw her, how much I missed Jess' mischievous smile, which had not been scraped away by adulthood, but had refined itself into a worldly smirk, the grin of a girl who always knew exactly who the joke was on. Not this time, though, she still didn't know. Didn't know about me, or Little Lecie, or the Pervert, the last of whom had slunk back into my mind the moment Derek and I passed the Old Winthrop Road on our way into town.

"So you guys were pretty good friends with her?" Chad asked. He sat half-turned with his arm along the back of the booth behind Jess' shoulders. They looked like college sweethearts home for Thanksgiving break. Me, envious.

"Until junior high," Jessica said. "Then, you know, in junior high you make new friends."

"But you two stayed friends," Chad said, indicating Jess and I.

"Lecie though," Jess said, staring out the window and shaking her head. "She was one of those girls who turned wild in high school. Like, out of control. And she was never like that. Was she, Emma?"

"Not as a kid, no," I said.

"Wild how?" Chad asked.

Derek said nothing, watching over me to see if I might crack. But cracking was not something I would do. Soul like Maine limestone.

"Drugs," Jess said. "Drugs get some people up here. There ain't shit else to do." Hamming up the Downeast accent. "We had, like, what, maybe three, four classmates get pregnant in high school and drop out? Lecie was one. I think the father was Aaron Wilkerson, a real prince from Clayton's trailer kingdom. He was like five years older. Fresh off the farm from an assault charge. She had another kid a year later. With somebody else."

With Jessica as narrator, the story of Lecie's life read like a rap sheet. Or a rap song. I decided not to contribute a verse. In high school Lecie had been a cutter, and her parents had put her in an institution in Lewiston. In one of the rare conversations Lecie and I had in high school she told me she used to piss herself in the hospital because the drugs made her so groggy she could not get out of bed. And there was a female nurse there who used to fondle her at night. Allegedly. I cried when I heard that story. Cut myself too, with an Exacto knife.

Outside the sky was steel gray. Leaves swept down the street in great, migratory flocks. The thin coffee at Millie's would never win a taste contest. It was hot though, and I sipped it quickly, inviting the burn.

"I always felt sorry for her mom," Jess continued. "Brenda really tried to help. She took the kids after the state tried to take them away from Lecie."

With a dull feeling of repressed panic I realized that Lecie's kids, now young adults themselves, would be at the funeral.

"It will be good to see Brenda again," I said quietly.

Derek gave me the checking-on-you look. I nodded and leaned against him.

"It's like there were two types of people up here," Jessica said. "The ones who grew up and went to college." She waved her hand to indicate herself and I. "And the ones who just did drugs. And it's so strange, because if you think back to, like, kindergarten, elementary school, we were all the same. We all played tag and soccer, and watched *The Simpsons*. You wonder how people end up taking such different paths."

"Were drugs really that much of a problem?" Chad asked. "Seems pretty quaint out here. This isn't exactly *Breaking Bad*."

"Well, everybody smokes weed," Jess said. "Everybody *grows* weed. And like I said, there's nothing really to do, and it's so damn dark all the time. Kids were doing 'shrooms, and acid, and coke. Then Oxy and meth." She shuddered. "Makes it kinda hard to come back here."

"And Lecie just fell in with the wrong crowd?"

It was like Jess and Chad were having their own conversation. So many couples seemed to form a shell. Maybe I was going to crack.

"I don't know if drugs were the problem for Alecia," I said. "They might have been the symptoms. I think a demon got her."

"Apparently," Jessica agreed, but she had no idea what I was talking about.

We had to leave for the funeral in a few minutes, and I definitely wasn't going to bring up the Pervert.

The same inglorious summer as the antique shop sneak I was out riding my bike alone, something I often did when

I wanted to think. The long empty roads around Clayton wound up and down rolling green hills. I pedaled hard up the hills, thighs burning, teeth clenched, then cruised down, exhilarated, wild, gliding to a gentle stop.

Since peering into the abyss of the Book, sex had been on my mind. In school they had taught us the nuts and bolts, so to speak, in a grossly selective, Christian-flavored affront to sexual education that left most of us (I imagine) with more questions than answers. My peek at the Book told me there were questions far beyond the scope of sex ed. I had developed a crush on a boy that summer; Tom Higgins, a kid who threw pebbles at younger kids on the playground. And that was the summer of the Pervert.

Everyone in Clayton was in a thinly-veiled huff about Albert French, who had inherited his deceased parents' dilapidated farmhouse out on the Old Winthrop Road. I don't know how the grim truth of Albert's past first leaked, but I remember my mother coming home from a PTA meeting in a steely-eyed tizzy, her limbs flailing with more angry conviction than usual. "Well, we have a child-molester living in Clayton," she told my father. The rumor mill churned out the rest. He had exposed himself, he had touched a girl, he had touched a boy, he had done time, he had not done time, he had been institutionalized, he was on parole. Small-town speculation.

None of us kids had ever seen the Pervert. No one knew what he looked like. But we kept our eyes peeled around town. And we knew where he lived.

I was still on my invincible girl streak. My older sister Corey was in eighth grade, and had dated two boys, and claimed to know everything about boys. She talked incessantly about her boyfriends. She literally ran to answer the phone when it rang. And I went for bike rides thinking about the penises I had glimpsed in the Book, my heart clenched in a tight, nervous fist. The penises had scared me, especially in the image where the woman was gleefully gripping two of them, but they also excited me, and I desperately wanted to see one, if only to wipe that know-it-all grin off my sister's face.

To make matters worse, Jessica had already seen a penis, three weeks earlier, at a birthday pool party I had missed because I was grounded for sneaking into the antique shop. Bobby Callahan took down his bathing suit behind the pool when the other kids were swarming the birthday cake, and since then Jess' mischievous grin lingered a little too excruciatingly long when she smiled at me.

I sort of knew what I was doing when I pedaled my bike up the Old Winthrop Road, and I sort of had no fucking clue. The Pervert lived on the downslope of a hill, a small house set back from the road. It badly needed painting. I imagined myself the very picture of bravery as I prepared to ride by, the little girl defying the Pervert. Jess would not have dared ride her bike up the Old Winthrop Road- and chicken-hearted Little Lecie? Forget about it.

I lost my nerve as I cruised down the hill, just before I passed the crooked mailbox. Panic seized my chest and I pedaled hard in low gear, tripping up my feet. The handlebars swerved in my sweaty grip and I veered into the ditch, held on as I hit the embankment, but lost the bike and vaulted over the stone wall. I may have blacked out for a split-second, and I remember feeling grateful that on that occasion I was wearing a helmet. Both my knees were torn and bleeding. I don't know how long I sat in the tall grass, not crying but more like scolding myself.

"Looks like you took a spill."

I was more embarrassed than scared as I looked up. He stood about ten feet away, arms crossed, wearing grass-stained jeans, a flannel shirt, unlaced boots. I thought the boots being unlaced was strange.

"Come on inside, I'll fix you up," he said.

"No- no thanks," I mumbled. "I'll just ride home."

"Come on."

"It's okay."

"You don't want to get infected. Come on now, won't take a second. We'll get the dirt out, and you won't bleed all over your clothes."

Two thin strands of blood ran down my legs. I had little conviction around adults at eleven- every child's inherent weakness. I followed him into the house, leaving the bike propped against the stone wall at the end of his driveway. I did not think I would ever see my bike again.

Inside the house smelled of dirt and mold, and saw dust. He was fixing up the place, one room at a time. There was dry wall in the kitchen, exposed insulation in the foyer. He told me to sit at the kitchen table. The chair creaked on the floor as I sat down.

He didn't say much as he cleaned my knees, warning me, as adults always did, that the alcohol would sting. Firmly he swept the dirt out of my cuts. He asked me my name and I told him, my heart pounding. I had no idea what was going to happen. After applying broad square bandages to my knees he threw the bloody gauze in the trash and washed his hands in the sink.

"Always wash your hands after you touch blood," he told me. "They teach you that in school?"

"I don't know."

"I'll bet your blood is clean as a whistle though," he said.

He smiled at me for what seemed like a long moment, and that was when I knew I should run. But I didn't. I felt glued to the chair. I hunched my shoulders and pulled my knees together.

"Sit still a minute, I'm going to go get something," he said, and his tone of voice had shifted.

I stared at the floor. I could feel my heartbeat in my ears.

He returned about two minutes later, and at first I had the weird sensation that it might be a dream. Like the whole day might be a dream. That might make sense. He stood there naked except for his dirty unlaced boots, his face the grin of a fiend, his penis swollen and erect. It was like the drawings in the Book, but real, pink and fleshy and not something that could be banished with the turn of a page.

The only thing I could think was: how would I explain this to my parents? First the Book, now this. They had threatened to send me to a therapist after the antique shop incident, but ultimately settled on a firm grounding instead. Now they would know there was something wrong with me. My whole life was about to end.

"I helped you, now you're going to help me."

He took a step toward me. I imagined my mother yelling at me.

My mouth was bone dry, but somehow I whispered "I don't think so," and I jumped from the table. The chair clattered to the floor. I bounded outside and sprinted for my bike, thinking that the steep slope of the hill was my getaway, the only thing that would save me. My footsteps dragged along like his driveway was wet cement.

At the end of the driveway I jumped onto my bike. I had no idea where my helmet was now. Maybe it was still in his house.

"Hey!"

I looked up, pushing the bike into the road.

Now in bare feet, wearing only his jeans, he stomped toward me. I stood frozen in the road, staring at this strange approaching beast. He stopped too, pointing at me, his eyes scowling black.

"I know you," he said. "I will find you. I helped you and you owe me. You know you owe me."

For some reason that I could explain, I knew what he meant. I was escaping, but with a debt. I felt like he could see into my soul. Even if I made it home, I knew there was nowhere I could hide. I'd been stamped with the mark of the demon.

"You will give me something," he growled. "Or I will find you."

I released the hand breaks of my bike and pedaled for all my skinny, blood-streaked legs were worth. In moments I was flying down the hill, back toward town, away from the Pervert and his saw dust hovel.

Later I told my parents I had wiped out coming down a hill too fast, and had bandaged my knees myself.

It was a closed casket funeral. I did not want to contemplate what Alecia Farmer's face might look like after she had hung herself and been found dead hours later.

Derek and I sat with Jess and Chad in the back of the Clayton Universalist Church. The minister spoke a few somber words about Lecie. Suicide cast an extra shade of darkness on the occasion. It had been the same way at my ex-roommate's funeral, after she killed herself. Nobody said anything. The cause of death hung over the room like Death's own scythe, ready to fall on everyone.

Lecie's mother Brenda sat in the first row, next to Lecie's father, Chuck. They were divorced and had each remarried. Brenda's face had swollen and grayed over the years. She looked like a woman without a soul.

I could not help staring at the backs of the heads of the young man and woman sitting beside Brenda. The young man had long hair dangling in greasy rebellion from his head, like Curt Cobain. He wore a black suit, pinstriped. Beside him sat the girl, her hair buzzed into one of those half-shaved punk styles, her ears pierced several times. These were Lecie's children, and I tried desperately to avoid making assumptions about them. Would they or did they already follow in Lecie's footsteps? Had the next generation been contaminated too? I could feel my chest tightening. I squeezed Derek's hand, tried to think of something else.

What I did think about were the words of the Pervert on the day I narrowly escaped his grasp. "I will find you." The standing threat. The demon always did find you, didn't it?

While Alecia Farmer was getting high and fucking random men through her misguided youth, I had tried to be careful with sex. Tried to maintain control. Lecie became one of those kids parents warned you about in high school- don't end up like her. Personally I was determined never to become Lecie. She and I were fundamentally different, and I knew why. I harbored terrified illusions of superiority, and I chose my boyfriends carefully.

Until college, when everyone goes a little haywire. There was so much drinking and so much talk of sex that every weekend when I joined the hoards of roaming partiers I felt like a driver on a midnight highway with my headlights off. Thrilled and reckless and curious to see how fast I could go without crashing.

On a college night like any other the demon caught up with me. Drunk, giddy, I followed my boyfriend back to his dorm room. There, playing video games was his roommate, drunk as well. My boyfriend insisted on making out on his bed, and I did not object, despite the roommate. I had never been watched before, was not entirely opposed to it, figured drunkenly that that was something kinky I could hold over everyone else. But his roommate turned off his video games and then he was on the bed with us, and soon we were performing a sloppy version of the picture I had seen in the Book so many years before. Me naked on the bed, holding them in my hands. The next morning I did not tell anyone about it, or brag to girlfriends later, but I owned the experience, just another one of life's punches- it stung for a while, then went away.

Everyone was invited to the cemetery after the service to see Lecie's coffin lowered into the ground. The crowd milled around in the sanctuary, mostly silent.

"I don't know if I can go," I whispered to Jess.

"I think we can leave," she said, nodding at Chad for confirmation. "We should say something to Brenda first."

I was grateful for Derek's grip on my hand as we walked toward Lecie's mother. It was a good life we'd built, I thought, and soon I would be back to it, hiding in front of my television.

A part of me wanted to confess the truth to Brenda, and I could feel it leaking out of my brain, ready to be spoken. But as we reached her I realized it would be absurd and cruel to add to her pain, a needless kick while she was down.

"Oh, look at you girls," Brenda said, squeezing Jessica and I by our arms. "I appreciate your coming. I know Alecia would have too."

"I suppose we could have been around more since the old days," I managed to say.

Brenda took me in her arms and hugged me, a gesture I was not ready for, and in no way deserved.

"Your being here now is what matters," she said.

The hug was suffocating. I needed her to let go or I was going to cry. Finally she released me, and I retreated to Derek's side, laced my fingers through his.

"Maybe we could get together for a visit sometime," Jessica said, placing her hand on Brenda's arm. "You know, to remember Alecia the way we want to."

So grateful for Jess, and her oblivious well-meaning.

"I would like that," Brenda said. "You girls were such good friends to Lecie when you were little."

Brenda said goodbye and turned to other mourners. Jess took her husband by the hand and ferried our group toward the door.

"You drive," I said to Derek when we reached the parking lot.

"Just come with me and all is forgiven."

For weeks after I escaped from the Pervert I could not relax or sleep. I lay in bed, expecting him to jump out of the closet or out from under the bed, like some monster. I slunk around the house, checking to make sure the doors were always locked. I left lights on at night, wore layers of clothes even though it was not cold. My parents asked me if I was behaving strangely to get attention. There was more talk of sending me to a therapist.

When you're a kid you believe the monsters. It never occurred to me to tell my parents what had happened. As an adult I knew that if I had told my parents a convicted sex offender had exposed himself to me and threatened me, the police would have been over to his house that day, and he might have gone to jail. But as a girl I just assumed he was lying in wait for me in some shadow, a coiled snake.

"You owe me something."

The words repeated themselves endlessly in my head, a snarling voice I could not tell to shut up. I came to realize that if I was ever going to escape from the monster, I would have to do what it wanted.

I met Lecie on a cool Sunday afternoon. School had started, and everyone seemed to have a boyfriend except me. Jess was going out with Bobby Callahan, the poolside penis-shower. Even Little Lecie had a boy interested in her. While I remained distrustful of boys. Jess and Lecie did not know what I knew. Jess only knew about the Book. And Lecie the baby knew nothing.

We rode our bikes out of town. At first I tried to talk to her, mostly to relax myself, but my chest felt packed with ice.

"I thought you were mad at me, Emma," she said. "About the antique shop."

"It was nothing," I said. "Just come with me and all is forgiven."

Eventually I just shut up and pedaled.

When we reached the Old Winthrop Road, I leaned into the turn and pedaled harder. Lecie picked up her pace and followed me. Poor dumb Lecie, she really had no idea what demons lurked out there in the world. She was one of those girls who cried when she got in trouble, fingered somebody else to take the blame, and got away with things, learning nothing. She needed to know that sometimes you had to face the bad things, that nobody was going to bail you out.

I stopped at the end of the Pervert's driveway, sweating and out of breath from the uphill climb. I wished I had remembered to bring a water bottle. My swollen tongue filled my mouth.

"How much further are we going?" she asked after a few minutes.

"Let's just take a break here."

A moment later he appeared, not from the front door of his house, but from the brambles out by his woodshed. He wore dirty overalls and work boots. Staggered across his weedy lawn and down his driveway like some forest creature. He waved when he saw me, smiling as if we were old buddies. I waved back.

"Who is that?" Lecie asked.

"Just the man who lives here," I said. "He's nice. Remember when I wiped out and skinned my knees? He bandaged me up. I would have had to go to the doctor."

Lecie looked skeptical as he approached, covering her eyes to shield out the autumn sun.

"Hi there, Emma," he said.

Of course he remembered my name. My heart was pounding, a dull feeling of nausea sloshing around in my stomach.

"Hello," I said.

"You girls out for a bike ride? Nice day."

We nodded.

"You look thirsty. Don't you have any water?"

"Forgot it, I guess," I said.

"You should always bring water when you go out for a ride. Don't want to dehydrate. Didn't they teach you that in school?"

"I don't know," we both kind of said at the same time.

"You want to come inside? I've got a pitcher of lemonade."

Lecie glanced at me nervously. She looked dubious of the muddy man from the dilapidated farmhouse, but also I could tell she was thirsty. She would follow my lead.

"Okay," I said, my voice barely a whisper.

He grinned and waved us toward his house. We walked our bikes behind him. I could think of nothing but the monster, so I started singing some inane song I could not remember now for the life of me, and this must have relaxed Lecie a little bit.

"Go ahead park your bikes against the house," he said.

Lecie leaned hers against the paint-peeling wall. I rested mine over hers.

He opened his door and stood in the doorway. Inside there was little light. Lecie stepped inside, still wearing her helmet. I stood perfectly still in the driveway. They both turned and stared at me.

"Emma?" he said. "Lemonade?"

"I... have to get home," I said. "I'll get some later."

Distrust filled Lecie's eyes. He gently took her hand and closed the door, nodding at me as he did so. I nodded too. We had an understanding. The monster was appeased.

I pedaled home and went into the bathroom and threw up. My parents were not home. I had no idea where they were. I went up to my room and shut the door and sat on my bed, crying. Over time that day just became one more thing I never told anyone.

On our way out of Clayton after the funeral I told Derek to turn onto the Old Winthrop Road. It was not exactly the right way home, but it was not out of the way either.

"I haven't been through town in so many years," I said, as if I just wanted to take the scenic route to check out the autumn leaves. Derek shrugged and turned up the road.

At some point when I was in high school they caught the Pervert. He was sent to Thomaston for some act of indecency.

Derek drove past the Pervert's old house without turning his head, but I glanced over, briefly. Long enough to see the faded "For Sale" sign at the end of the driveway, the boards on the windows, a red sign posted over the door.

About two weeks later I told Derek I was meeting a co-worker for dinner and a movie, a woman named Dinah, whom I did occasionally go out with so we could drink wine and gripe about work. Derek casually waved me off, an evening of TV and fantasy football ahead of him.

I drove out to Clayton. My mind raced with a checklist of silly precautions gleaned almost entirely from television shows. Had I remembered to fill my car with gas? Yes, that explained my trip to the gas station three days ago, my purchase of gasoline. Had I wore a dark, non-descript outfit? Yes, jeans and a coat I almost never wore. Had anyone seen me leaving town? No.

I thought of Brenda hugging me at Lecie's funeral. The poor oblivious woman, whose life had been ransacked by her daughter's behavior for twenty years, even before the suicide. Never knowing what the cause of it all was. And I the coward, failing to tell her the truth. Standing there in an embrace I did not deserve while her daughter lay in a closed casket.

I parked on the Old Winthrop Road in the dark, not pulling into the ditch, where my tires would leave tracks. I took off my shoes so I would not leave footprints, ran down the Pervert's driveway in my thick socks. In my gloved hands I carried the can of gasoline. From television I knew that an astute investigator would find traces of gasoline in the refuse, evidence of an "accelerant," implying arson. A risk I was willing to take. I would throw away this entire outfit, everything I was wearing, in some random dumpster in Lewiston on the way home, change into the spare outfit I had in the car.

I poured gasoline all around the frame of the Pervert's house. I thought about kicking in a window and throwing the can in too, then thought no, I would dispose of it in another dumpster, different from the one for the clothes. There was little time. Someone could come down the road, see my car. I bent to the base of the wall and lit the gasoline with a disposable lighter. The gas erupted in a hot puff, swallowing the cold night air. The old damp rotten wood took a moment to catch, but then suddenly a ring of fire engulfed the house.

I'm sorry, Lecie, that I sacrificed you to the demon. I wish I could pull you back from that house, bring you home safe to Brenda, tell you I loved you.

I drove away in the dark, heart pounding, bowels a bowl of cold water, devilish flames dancing in the rearview.

Chapter 7

Just the Usual Horses

Maine, 1881

Daniel stood at the back door, watching the barn, boots caked with dirt from the fields. His chores weren't done yet. He still had to feed the horses.

In the dining room, silverware scraped the wooden table. He could smell his mother's stew: rabbit and potatoes and carrots. He was starving. But as he stared out at the evening darkness, at the barn looming like a gray ghost, his appetite slithered away. November was a dark month. Fiery leaves had fallen, coating the hard ground, leaving skeletal trees to fend for themselves.

"Daniel." Father's hand on his shoulder. "Supper arrives. Tend the horses, son."

"Father, there's something out there, spooking the horses," Daniel said.

"Enough of that."

"These last few nights especially."

"I said enough."

Daniel heard footfalls on the soft wood, knew Rachel was listening somewhere.

"Rachel," Father said. "No eavesdropping."

"I wasn't."

"You'll help Daniel in the barn. Hurry, ye both. Supper arrives."

Rachel clomped across the floor, stepped into the work boots perched by the door. Daniel stepped outside and headed for the barn. He did not need his sister's help.

"Daniel, wait."

He walked straight for the barn, and she ran after him. "I said, wait."

She caught up with him, and together they went into the barn. Daniel set the lantern down on the work bench, painting warm strokes of light across the barn's towering crossbeams. There were three stalls, one for each of their horses. He pulled two of them open, and Rachel opened the third.

"I can get the door," she said.

"Oats first."

They found the sack of oats beneath the work bench, lifted it together to pour a cascade of dry food into the feeding trough of each stall. At eleven, Daniel could just reach the wall-mounted troughs. Rachel, a year younger, grunted under the weight of the feed sack.

"Don't spill," Daniel said.

"I never spill."

They replaced the feed sack, walked to the broad, swinging door to the horse pasture. Daniel grabbed the cold iron handle and yanked the door open. It rumbled on its iron hinges, a deep sound like rocks shifting under water. They stood in the light of the doorway, staring out at the pasture. The night stared back at them like an expressionless face, a huge open mouth ready to swallow.

"Come on, y'dumb beasts!" Daniel called. "Come git it!"

"They ain't dumb," Rachel whispered.

"Hush."

Eventually they heard the clopping of hooves. Two of the horses materialized out of the mist. Rolly, the workhorse, and Misty, the gray mare, loped toward the barn. Daniel and Rachel stood aside. The horses jogged past them like giants. Each found its way into its stall.

"Come on now, where's Chester," Daniel said. He did not want to go out into the pasture to look for their aged third equine, Chester, the retired work horse their father just could not bring himself to shoot.

"Chester!" Rachel called.

"Hush."

"Hush, what? What are you scared of?" She glared at him defiantly. "I'll go out there and get 'im."

"No," he said. "We'll go together."

He retrieved the lantern from the work bench.

"I can see in the dark," Rachel said as they padded out into the pasture.

"That's witch talk."

"No, it ain't. I'm just not scared, like you."

"You're simple."

The barn receded into darkness behind them. Beneath their feet the grassy fields were slick with autumn mud. Daniel glanced back at the farmhouse, the twin glowing lights of the kitchen and dining room. He wished he was inside.

"Chester," he said, firmly. "Come git it."

They stood perfectly still. Daniel squinted into the darkness. As his vision adjusted, the pasture expanded around them, a pool of deep shadows. There were stars above, but no moon. Across the field he could distantly make out the stone wall at the edge of the farm. Beyond which lay the endless sprawl of the forest.

Something moved by the stone wall. "I see him," Daniel said.

"I don't see-"

Suddenly Chester chugged out of the night, nearly crashing into them. Daniel jumped out of the way. The horse huffed, thundering toward the barn, oblivious.

"You old dingbat!" Rachel cried.

Daniel shuddered, glancing back toward the stone wall. Rachel stood still, pointing to the distant line of trees. "You said you saw him over there."

"I thought I did."

"But he came from this way," she indicated with her thumb. "What'd you see?"

Daniel looked at her. "Come on," he said. "Father won't be kept waiting."

He turned and walked back toward the barn. After a moment she followed.

"You're telling lies," Rachel said. "Father's right about your fibbing."

Daniel grabbed the lapel of her blouse. She stiffened, her hands clenching into fists. "I don't tell lies," Daniel said. He let go of her blouse, stalked into the barn.

She hurried after him.

There was fog for a week, every morning and every afternoon, each day a little darker than the last. Rachel spent long hours with Mother, peeling and canning potatoes, skinning the papery lumps until her hands cramped into painful claws.

"Mother, how long do we have to eat potatoes?" she asked.

Mother sliced the peeled potatoes into chunks. Mary, Rachel's younger sister, shoved the chunks into jars.

"Until May, if we're lucky," Mother said.

"My hands are soon to fall off."

"Finish your pile. Then bring in the dry linens."

Rachel wished she was in the orchard with Father and the boys, picking apples for the cider. Eating fresh apples off the trees. Not skinning dirty little ground turds for the evening stew. She peeled through her pile, then set down the paring knife. "I'll get the linens now," she said.

Outside, another foggy afternoon bled into evening. Rachel pulled her coat around her shoulders, buttoned it at the neck.

The linens sagged from the clothes line, damp and heavy, always damp this time of year. She would hang them by the fire to dry during supper, but her bed would still be wet and cold.

One of the horses trotted through the fog, appearing like a half-formed thought, vanishing.

"Chester, where are you going?" she mumbled. But the horse had not looked like Chester. It was deep brown, not auburn-gray.

Rachel left the linen hanging, walked out into the pasture. Gray swirls of mist circled around her. She walked across the field, where the horse had gone. She arrived at the corner of the stone wall, and stopped short. Daniel stood facing the woods, his back to her.

"Daniel, you scared me," Rachel said.

He did not respond. She stepped toward him. "Daniel...."

"I heard you. Hush."

She stood beside him. His face was pinched and alert, his eyes narrow, scanning the trees.

"What are you doing out here?" she whispered.

He turned to her. "What are you?"

"I saw a horse, and I don't think it was Chester." She felt her chest tighten. "I think it was a horse."

"Brown-colored. Like dirt?"

"Yes."

He raised a thin finger, pointing into the trees. Rachel squinted, saw nothing. A wisp of cold air nipped at her cheeks. She stepped closer to him, her fingers fumbling at the hem of his coat. "Is Father keeping Mr. Crother's horse for him, like last summer?" she whispered.

"No," Daniel said.

She followed the direction of his finger. In the trees, a shape moved. It was nearly indistinguishable from the trunks.

"That's a deer," she said. "Let's tell Father. We'll eat venison till Christmas!"

She started to turn, but he grabbed her arm. "It ain't a deer," he said. "It's a horse. A ghost horse. It's what's been spooking ours."

Rachel pulled away from his grasp. "It ain't a ghost horse," she stammered. "And you're fibbing again, just like Father says. I'm going to tell him it's a deer!"

She ran back across the field, heading straight for the house. She knew her father was in the orchard, picking apples, but she wanted to be away from the pasture. Distantly she heard the soft whinny of a horse, and she ran faster.

"I saw the brown horse again today," Daniel said, as they sat down to dinner. "Rachel saw it too."

Rachel kept silent, watching their father. Father's eyes closed for a moment, his whiskery jaws chewing slowly.

"Daniel," he said. "We have but three horses on this property. Always have had."

"I think there may be another," Daniel said.

"What you're doing is causing trouble," Father said. "I've seen no such horse. Your mother-" He turned to Mother for confirmation, and Mother curtly shook her head. "Your mother's seen no such horse. I've told you repeatedly about lies. Now account for your behavior."

Daniel glanced at Rachel. She stared down at her stew. The younger children watched them both.

"Every night when I feed the horses, they're restless," Daniel said. "I went to the barn yesterday, found tracks all over the place. No shoes on the tracks, Father. Our horses are shoed."

"If Crother was missing a horse, he'd be over," Father said.

"I might have seen a deer today, Father," Rachel said.

Father turned to her. "You see one again, you come find me."

"Yes, sir."

"Daniel," Father said. "I'll hear the Lord's prayer in triplicate from you, before bed time. And I'll hear you ask forgiveness for telling lies. There are no strange horses on this property. Just the usual ones."

That night Daniel lay in the children's bed, brooding. He didn't like his father to think he wasn't truthful. They were taught in Church to tell the truth, to respect their elders, and Daniel took pride in his inclination to do both. Reverend Wilkes had never called him a liar. Tomorrow he would find the brown horse and prove his virtue.

He kicked Rachel beneath the damp bedsheets. "That was not a deer, you simple idiot," he whispered.

Rachel kicked him back. "It was," she said. "You're blind as a fool."

"You saw a horse. You said so."

Rachel squirmed away from him. The other children breathed deeply in the bed.

"You're just trying to scare me," she huffed.

"You'll be sorry you didn't believe me," Daniel said. "When the ghost horse tramples you in your sleep."

He turned away from her. After a moment he heard her muffled whimpers, and he felt even worse.

After chores, Daniel stuffed four apples into his coat pockets. He went into the barn, retrieved the spare lantern his father hung above the work bench. He pocketed a tinder box and a pouch of gunpowder. It was another foggy afternoon. He had been watching the pastures all day, had seen a large brown shape flitting across the stone wall, leaping into the woods. He was half-convinced that Rachel was right- it was a deer they had seen- but he would not tell her so. Not until he had ventured into the forest and found the creature. If it was a deer, he would delight in watching Father shoot it.

"What are you doing with the lantern?"

Daniel turned and saw Rachel peering at him from one of the horse stalls.

"How come you're always where you ain't wanted?" Daniel replied. "Father told you not to eavesdrop."

She stepped out of the stall, hands on her hips. "Father told you not to fib."

"Father told you not to piss in the yard."

Rachel's mouth dropped open. "I'll piss anywhere I please," she said. "What are you stealing the tinderbox for?"

"I ain't stealing. I'm going to look for the horse."

"What horse?"

"The ghost horse."

"That was a deer."

"Now *you're* fibbing."

Rachel ran up to him. "I don't want you wandering around in the woods. It'll be dark soon."

"That's why I'm bringing the lamp."

"I won't have it."

"You, you, you." He pushed her chest. "You can stay here, yard-pisser. I'm going to find the horse. I won't be called a liar by Father, by you, or by anyone."

He walked out of the barn, glanced around to make sure Father wasn't watching out for him. Father was across the pastures, deep in the orchard, picking the cider apples. Mother was in the house teaching Mary and John their lessons. The pasture was gray and empty, fog curling out of the forest. He expected to hear Rachel's footsteps following him after about ten paces, and when he glanced back around, there she was.

Wet sticks crunched beneath their boots. The forest was coffin still. Black trees tilted around them, hemming them in. Tendrils of fog curled through the damp air. Daniel wished he hadn't brought the lantern. It was needlessly heavy, though he'd be grateful for it if they didn't find the horse by dark.

"How do you know I piss in the yard?" Rachel griped. "You must be watching me."

"Everyone knows," Daniel said. "Reverend Wilkes sermoned about it Sunday last."

"Liar!"

"Father says only men can piss outside. It ain't ladylike."

"Mother says it helps kill the crab grass."

"Mother does not talk about such things."

"She does too," said Rachel. "When you and Father and John are in the fields."

"Well, I'll not have you pissing in the yard if we're married someday," Daniel said.

Rachel scoffed. "Brothers don't marry sisters. That ain't how marriage works, ya ignoramus."

A nickering sound broke the stillness of the woods. Daniel froze. Rachel bumped into him. She grabbed his coat. "What was that?"

Daniel scanned the trees. Gnarly brown trunks in every direction.

"It wasn't a deer," he said.

They stood still. Something cracked nearby. Daniel swung around.

The horse stood twenty yards away, head bent forward. Pawing the dirt. Canon blasts of breath exploded from its nostrils.

Daniel felt his heartbeat in his ears. The horse shook its heavy mane.

Rachel stepped behind him. "Daniel-"

"Hush-"

It charged them. Rachel screamed. Daniel pulled them both to the ground. The horse pounded through the trees. Branches snapped against its chest. He could smell its musky bulk, felt a rush of air brush his face. There was a moment of silence as the horse leapt over their crouching form. It landed inches from Rachel's dress, took off at a gallop into the woods.

Rachel clung to him. "Is it gone?"

"I don't know where it is."

"I want to go home."

"We'll go. Take my hand."

She gripped his hand so tight it hurt. Daniel held the lantern out in front of them, like a weapon. Their only defense, and not even lit. Darkness was closing in.

He realized he had no idea which way led back to the farm. They could not see the pastures through the trees. He knew that the sun set south and west in autumn, but there was no sun, just a thick wall of fog.

They climbed over a fallen trunk, their feet sinking deep into soft dirt.

"Now I'm stuck," Rachel said.

The horse stood fifty feet away, perfectly still. Rachel gasped, a whisper of breath escaping her mouth.

It stared right at them.

"Run," Daniel said.

"I can't! I'm stuck!"

He dropped the lantern, grabbed her ankles, and wrenched her feet out of the muck. She fell backwards with a cry. He pulled her up, and they sprinted into the trees. Rachel's legs tangled in her dress, but he did not release her hand. He would not abandon his sister.

Galloping footsteps thundered behind them. The horse whinnied madly, the wild cry of a crazed thing. They ducked their heads and ran faster. Daniel's breath choked in his throat. Beside him he heard Rachel crying.

They tripped over wet branches, crashing to the ground. Daniel felt his ankle twist. Rachel stood up, lurched forward, fell again, her dress clinging to her legs.

"Stop," Daniel said.

She stopped, breathing hard. He grabbed a low tree branch and pulled himself to his feet. The forest was dark, the mist closing around them like a fist.

"Where is it?" she asked.

He looked around. He could see nothing, could barely see Rachel a few feet away. But the forest smelled funny. Like a barn. Like-

The horse nickered beside them.

He grabbed her again and ran, this time in no direction at all. His ankle smarted with each crashing step. Branches snagged their clothes, nicked their faces. They pushed through a clump of thick brambles, fell forward into a clearing.

"Daniel, what is that?"

Daniel caught his breath and stood. A rotten barn stood before them, tucked into the edge of the clearing. He had never seen the barn before. He and Father had walked all over their property, in summer, when the forest was golden green and alive. The barn croaked out of the forest floor like a tomb, its doorless maw a gaping black mouth.

"What is this place?" Rachel asked.

"I don't know," Daniel said. "Let's go inside. We can hide."

They ran into the barn. It was smaller than their own barn, much smaller, just a single square room with a loft above. A rotten table and chair sat in the middle of the room. A frayed rope hung from the rafters. They leaned against the wall. Listened.

Outside they heard a coarse whinny, not the sound of a healthy animal, but the rasping breath of decay.

Daniel found a rotten ladder leading up to the loft. He squeezed the soft wood. "We can hide up there," he said.

He climbed, and Rachel followed. The loft was empty, but for a few brittle straws of hay. They huddled together on the thin wooden floorboards.

"Father will kill us," Rachel said. "If that monster don't kill us first."

"It can't get up here," Daniel said. "It can't climb a ladder."

"We'll miss supper, and the horses will go unfed."

Daniel stared out into the dark forest. He could see absolutely nothing. It would do no good to try to hike back to the farm. They would have to spend the night in the barn.

"We'll go home in the morning," he said, not at all confident that he could find the way. He wished he had not dropped the lantern. Without a lamp the tinderbox and powder in his pocket were useless. He reached into his coat and pulled out two apples, gave one to Rachel.

"Thank you," she said.

They ate in silence, then sat together, listening to the night. There was no wind, no rain, no owls. No footsteps or nickers. Nothing but the sound of their own breathing.

Eventually they lay down and tried to sleep. Daniel felt Rachel's shivering body, and he pulled her close against him. She smelled of damp hair, and potatoes. He kissed her forehead, and for a moment she stopped shivering, and soon she was asleep. Daniel closed his eyes.

He awoke to the gruff nicker of a horse.

"Easy," said a low male voice.

Daniel sat up. Rachel breathed gently beside him. He peered over her.

An orange glow emanated from the room below them. Daggers of light danced across the walls. A lantern.

"Easy," said the man again.

It was not Father. Daniel sat perfectly still.

The horse nickered again.

"You're on your own now," said the man. "Ye can have this cursed land all to ye'self. I'm done."

The man whispered something Daniel could not hear.

Rachel stirred. Opened her eyes. Daniel put a finger to his lips.

"I've failed myself, failed my family, and now I've failed you," the man said.

"Father?" Rachel whispered.

Daniel shook his head. Her eyes widened.

"Let's see *you* grow potatoes in that soil," the man said. "Let's see you grow *anything*. Maine soil ain't nothing but rocks. Should never have left Boston."

More mumbling. Daniel heard what sounded like liquid sloshing in a bottle.

"Well, I quit. I'm sorry to do this to you, old friend. But I quit."

There was a wooden groaning sound, like furniture moving around. Daniel heard the man reciting something quietly. It sounded like the Lord's prayer. Then there was a heavy tremor, and the barn shook. The horse nickered and whinnied. Pounded its hooves on the dirt floor. A rhythmic creaking seeped through the barn, like a ship bobbing at anchor.

Several minutes passed, and they heard no more sounds from the man or the horse.

"Don't move," Daniel said. He crawled to the edge of the loft, peered down into the room. He could not see the entire space, but there was a lantern, lit, and a table, with an empty chair. He followed the creaking sound, gazing up to the rafters. A rope dangled from the crossbeams, and a man hung from the rope. Boots swaying back and forth, just above the ground.

The horse stared directly at him. Blew steam from its nostrils. It seemed to be waiting for something.

Daniel crawled away from the edge of the loft.

"What is it?" Rachel asked.

"The man left," Daniel said.

"Is the horse still there?"

"Yes."

"Why?"

He lay back down beside her, pulled her close. "It can't get us up here," he stuttered, his lips like two pieces of ice. "We'll leave in the morning. Go back to sleep."

"I can't sleep with the demon down there."

"I won't let it get you."

She buried her face in his jacket. His lips found her ear, and he whispered Hail Mary's until they both fell asleep.

In the morning the barn was empty. No man hanging from the rafters. No lantern. No horse. No footprints on the dirt floor. They climbed down from the loft. Mercifully, the morning sun threw beams of light through the trees. Daniel knew the sun arced through the southern sky in autumn. He could find his way back to the farm.

They stepped outside the barn, and there was the horse. Watching them.

It looked smaller in daylight, older, its coat a faded brown. It pawed the ground listlessly, like it didn't know what else to do.

"What does it want?" Rachel asked.

Daniel remembered the words of the man from last night. "You're on your own now."

"It's hungry," he said. He reached into his pocket, found the two remaining apples. His stomach growled from his own hunger, but he stepped forward, held the apples out in his hand. The horse nickered and stepped toward them. Rachel grabbed Daniel's jacket.

"Be still," Daniel said.

The horse loomed over them, its snout fumbling over his fingers, its eyes like clouded marbles. It smelled of stale breath and rotten soil. It sniffed the apples, then gently opened its jaws. Daniel fed the apples into the horse's mouth, one and then the other. The fruit crunched in its teeth.

"He's just hungry," Daniel said.

The horse finished eating, and released a long breath. It turned and loped off into the forest. There was no mist this morning. Daniel and Rachel watched the horse vanish into the trees, there one moment, gone the next.

They found their way back to the farm before noon. Deep in the trees, Daniel stubbed his toe on something metallic, looked down to see the abandoned lantern. He picked it up. One less lashing from Father.

They emerged into the pasture, climbed over the stone wall. Chester loped across the paddock toward the barn. They could not see the other horses. Thin smoke trickled out of the farmhouse chimney.

"Father will wear out his belt tonight," Daniel said.

"I won't let him say you're fibbing," Rachel said. "If he calls you a fibber again, I'll tell him you ain't one."

Daniel stared off toward the barn. Their father emerged with a pitchfork. He saw the children, and stalked toward them. Rachel took his hand, and together they walked across the pasture, toward their father's uncomprehending wrath.

Chapter 8

Mercy Kill

My older brother Erik and I had always been loyal to each other when it came to girls, adhering to clear territorial boundaries, but the line blurred for Jenna. We grew up in the small, lakeside village of Jasper, Maine. Jenna was our neighbor. One year younger than Erik and one year older than me, she was my brother's first crush, and then mine. She taught each of us to kiss, showed each of us the difference between her body and ours, adopted the role of our third musketeer, carried our triumvirate into high school.

Camping was a tradition we three established when we were young. We would pitch an L.L. Bean tent at the end of our yard beside the lake, worm our way into our sleeping bags, tell ghost stories, eat wild strawberries and blackberries. Later we went skinny dipping and puffed pilfered cigarettes. As teenagers we ventured beyond the safety of the yard, hiking deep into the Maine woods, camping far from Jasper.

Jenna was in love with Erik but confused about how to pursue him. I knew this because she told me so when she was fifteen and I was fourteen. Though it excited me that I was the one she could tell her secrets to, her confession made me jealous. It gave my brother the upper hand in our lifelong competition for her affections. But Erik seemed to have no idea how to act on Jenna's feelings. Sometimes I wondered if he even knew how she felt.

Girls generally liked Erik. He was outgoing, happy in a shy way, somewhat naïve. I think they could sense some inner goodness in him, a rabbit-like innocence they wanted to coddle and protect.

Although Erik was older than me, I crossed all the lines of adolescence before he did. I stole beer, and consumed it enthusiastically. I smoked pot, with a group of older kids. I got laid, when I was fifteen, with a girl from the next town over who had gone to summer camp with us. I didn't tell Erik. Whenever my brother talked about sex he did so with a dreamer's optimism, as if it might happen to him someday, if he was lucky.

The summer I was fifteen, Jenna sixteen, and Erik seventeen, we took a camping trip to Somerset Country at the end of August, two weeks before the start of another school year. It would be our last year in high school together, before Erik graduated and went off to college.

Erik drove the hour and a half into Western Maine, piloting us off the map to the unincorporated territory owned by the logging companies. We parked in a small clearing at the end of a dirt road where we hoped no one would find the car, and hiked several miles into the woods. When we reached a small lake that reminded us of our own lake in Jasper, we stopped and set up camp.

The forest was thick with mosquitoes. I chopped down a dead tree with my hatchet and made a fire. Erik poked three knife-whittled sticks into the ground and stuck hot dogs on the ends of them, roasting supper while Jenna brewed tea. I rolled a joint, and we passed it around. We went skinny dipping under the stars. I ducked under the water to see Jenna. Her slender white body was a shining blur, and I wanted to wrap my arms around her, slide my skin against hers, whisper to her all the secrets we had shared since childhood. But while I was staring at Jenna beneath the water, she was staring at my brother.

At night we cooked s'mores, then poured a pan of water on the fire. We crawled into our tent, shimmied into our sleeping bags, and Erik soon fell asleep. He always fell asleep first. That was Erik's way, secure and oblivious, checking out each night with a clear conscience. I knew enough to stay awake when there was a girl present. Give her as much time as she needed to realize I was not asleep either.

Jenna squirmed in her sleeping bag. I shifted my body next to her. She responded, curling sideways toward me, away from Erik. She slid her hand over my sleeping bag. I unzipped the bag and allowed her inside. She got me off there in the dark, but that was all. We did not even kiss. She approached me with her hand, not her face, which I took as a sign of some buried loyalty to my brother. But now I knew I had the upper hand, and if I wanted to pursue Jenna I could. Finally she had given me some sort of permission.

The next morning Jenna and I did not talk about the explorations of the night. We communicated with quiet looks, not quite smiles, as we spent the day fishing and swimming and drinking the beers I had taken from my father's fridge in the garage.

In late afternoon the three of us lay together on the pine needles beside the lake, gazing up at the towering trees, listening to the rustle of wind in the branches.

"You know if someone came along and murdered us right now, our bodies might never be found," Jenna said.

I stared at her curiously. She always said weird things. We hadn't even smoked any pot.

"The killer could dig an unmarked grave," she continued. "Or animals would carry off our bones."

"I'd be more worried about the animals," Erik said. "A bear's more likely to come along than a killer."

"What if someone followed us?" Jenna said.

"You'd be in trouble," I said. "He'd shoot or bludgeon me and Erik, then afterwards he'd have his way with you."

I had no idea why I said this. I suppose I wanted to sound tough. That was my thing that summer. I was the tough brother.

"I'd go for his eyes," Jenna said. "Stick my thumbs way down in there, in the goo."

"You're a sicko," I said. She smiled.

"It would never come to that," Erik said, squinting up at the shadows between the trees.

"What do you mean?" she asked.

"The killer would not be able to overpower the three of us. If he went for you, Sean and I would tackle him."

Erik's assurance that he and I were a team, prepared to handle an assault from a wilderness killer, made me feel guilty for fooling around with Jenna the night before.

Jenna now smiled at Erik, ran her fingers through his shaggy hair. "Erik, I don't believe you could ever hurt someone, even for me or Sean."

"I could if I had to," Erik said.

I think Jenna heard the airplane first, because she sat up slightly, craned her neck, turned her ear to the forest.

"What's up?" I asked.

"Do you guys hear that?"

I could only hear the wind, and maybe a slight buzz somewhere that could have been an insect. The buzz turned into a choppy hum, and I sat up too. "I hear something....".

The noise vanished, then returned louder, a sputter and a pop.

Erik stood up and scanned the sky. The sound died again abruptly, then virtually exploded above us. A dark shadow flashed overhead and a shaky white object sailed above the trees. We ducked to the ground, shaken by the thunderous engine, which popped again like a gunshot. In the sky we saw a trail of black smoke.

Erik ran to the water's edge. Jenna and I followed. We stood on slippery rocks and watched in disbelief as a small airplane careened through the air.

"That's a Cessna," Erik said. I knew he would know what kind of plane it was. Those were the kinds of things Erik knew, little details that made girls like him, that made Jenna look at him now.

"It's going down," I said. And it was.

The wings tilted and swayed, the engine bloc coughed thick clouds of black smoke. We watched in stunned silence as the plane veered suddenly away from the water, back toward the trees. Then we lost sight of it.

For a moment all we could hear were birds in the forest. Then the ground shook and we heard a distant sound like firecrackers that I realized was the sound of tree branches snapping.

"He crashed," Erik said.

"What should we do?" Jenna asked.

"Call it in," I said.

"There's no cell reception. I lost my signal twenty miles from here," she said.

"Then we hike back to the car."

"It's two hours away," Erik said. "It will be almost dark by then. We need to see if anyone survived."

He started running through the forest. Jenna glanced at me, then hurried after him. I lingered behind, and during that moment alone I made the practical decision to grab a full bottle of water, and our hatchet.

The forest was thicker than it had seemed on our initial hike to the campsite. Fallen trees and uprooted stumps littered the ground. Sticks and brambles and low branches lashed out at our arms, legs and faces as we ran. I broke into a sticky sweat. Bugs offered no quarter, swarming my eyes and hair. I slapped at them, stumbling, grabbing trees for support.

Ahead of me Jenna jogged at a measured, agile pace. She was a track runner at school, with strong legs and good wind. She ran smoothly, and I stared at her. It was an unusual time for arousal, but I could feel my blood warming up. Her body in motion seemed to guide me through the forest.

Erik reached the crash site first. Looking up we saw the jagged white guts of severed trees. Branches hung to the ground like broken arms, the thick green pine from the canopy pungent of pitch. The plane stuck ass-up in the air, spewing smoke, and I heard the crackle of fire before I saw the orange gasoline flames.

Someone screamed from the wreckage. Jenna stopped and turned to me, out of breath, her face red and bleeding from a scratch, her eyebrows pitched in a tent of concern. I stumbled up close to her, stood beside her and stared at the wreckage.

The flames from the engine burned high, and I hesitated, worried that the whole thing would explode. I wanted to stand in front of Jenna, protect her from the eruption. But I could see a man trapped in the cockpit, blood covering half his face, desperately struggling to pull himself out of his seat before the flames engulfed him.

Erik jumped up on the plane's fractured wing, buried his head and arms in the smoking cockpit. Jenna grabbed my hand and squeezed. I opened my mouth to shout a warning, but my cries were lost over the roar of the fire, and the painful screams of the pilot.

Erik emerged a moment later, his torso, arms and face blackened from smoke. He grabbed the pilot by the waist and yanked him out of the cockpit. Jenna and I lunged forward. Erik brought the pilot to the ground and together we dragged him from the wreckage.

The plane did not explode. It burned down to a skeleton. We stood in the trees and watched as the fire burned itself out. The pilot lay unconscious at our feet.

Jenna knelt beside him. "He's hurt bad," she said. His legs were black and smoldering. The sick scent of charred flesh filled the air. I wanted to throw up, but managed to hold it in. Gently I sipped from the water bottle.

"Can we move him?" Jenna asked. The pilot's legs were bent at unnatural angles, and we could see a bloody splinter of bone poking through one of his arms.

Erik bent over him, listened to the man's shallow breathing, felt for a pulse.

"We're going to have to carry him," he said.

"What if he has spinal damage?" said Jenna.

"It doesn't matter," I said, feeling like I had to say something to help. "If he stays here he's going to die."

Erik pointed to the hatchet in my hand. "We can build a stretcher," he said.

I hacked at tree branches in a cold sweat, adrenalin surging through my veins. We dragged four limbs together into a crude rectangle, then realized we had nothing to bind the frame with, until Jenna suggested our shoe laces. The stretcher was shaky but our bindings held.

"Careful," Erik said as we all took hold of the pilot.

I wrapped my hands around the hot, melted flesh of the man's ankles, swallowed a fresh wave of nausea. Jenna held her breath and shoved the pilot's good arm, as Erik and I dragged him by his brittle clothes onto the stretcher.

The pilot woke up as we set him down, wailed in pain, his eyes pinched shut. Blood oozed from a head wound where bone was visible, and Jenna sacrificed her tee shirt for a tourniquet.

"Hold on, sir," Erik said. "I know it hurts, but we're going to get you some help."

The man groaned, his protestations of pain garbled and unintelligible.

"Sean, grab the stretcher," said my brother. We lifted, he at the pilot's head and I at the feet.

Jenna led the way back through the forest toward our campsite, stalking through the woods now in unlaced shoes, with only her bra to protect her pale skin from the onslaught of mosquitoes. I was amped up on adrenalin, and my muscles burned from the weight of the pilot, but I still felt slightly aroused to see her almost naked. She turned around every few seconds to make sure we were still behind her. I dug my feet into the earth and sloughed forward, my arms heavy like lead, sweat pouring down my face. The pilot continued to moan, his head thrashing from side to side, his screams filling the forest and drowning out everything until they seemed to be coming from inside my head.

"Set it down a moment," Erik said, and gratefully I dropped my end of the stretcher.

The pilot cried out as we set him on the ground. "Oh god it hurts it fucking hurts so bad please kill me I can't take it!"

Jenna knelt beside him, rubbed his good arm. He did not seem to notice her. We all took a drink of water and Erik offered some to the pilot, but the injured man spat it back up, and after three tries Erik gave up.

The pilot's legs looked like two well-done steaks, and smelled so awful I cannot describe the stench. He begged again for death, repeated a raspy, choking plea over and over.

"Let's move," Erik said, and we soldiered on through the forest.

"Are we going the right way?" Jenna asked, still leading us but stopping every few feet to get her bearings. "I can't tell where we are."

"We're going the right way," Erik said. "The lake is on our left. As long as we keep it on our left we'll reach the campsite."

I realized he was right, wondered how he could keep his bearings under such pressure. I wished I was the one providing Jenna assurances, providing us all some comfort or certainty. Jenna now walked beside Erik, supporting him as much as the stretcher, taking a branch to relieve some of his burden.

The stretcher gave out after an hour. One of the shoelaces snapped and the branches by the pilot's legs came apart, dropping his feet to the ground. He screamed in agony, a sound that paralyzed the three of us until it tapered off into a sickening fluid gurgle.

Jenna held the pilot's hand while Erik tried to repair the shoelace. It wouldn't reattach. I had no idea how far we had run from the campsite to reach the plane, but it seemed like we should have been back at our tent by now.

I sat in the dirt and tried to think, watched my brother hover over the pilot. Blood had soaked through the tee shirt wrapped around the man's head. He opened his wild eyes but it was impossible to tell if he could see anything.

"Don't worry, sir," Erik said, his voice surprisingly calm. "We're going to get you some help. It's a long hike, but just hold on."

Suddenly the man's hand shot out and latched onto Erik's shirt, pulling my brother nearly down on top of him.

"Please kill me," the pilot begged, his eyes blood-shot and primal. "Please, please, I can't take it oh my god it hurts so much please. Just fucking kill me...."

Erik nodded and repeated that we were going for help. The man screamed himself into a fit and then suddenly passed out. Erik checked to make sure he was still breathing.

"Let's go," he said. "Just hold the stretcher together."

Jenna came around the pilot and grabbed the branches where they had come apart. She stood beside me now and I saw that her bare skin was covered in scratches and welts. Sweat ran in dirty stains down her face. My own arms and legs and shirt were covered in dirt and blood and debris from the forest. Erik's face was red and strained, his hair dripping sweat. We heaved the stretcher off the ground and tried to move forward.

We made it a few hundred yards before another shoe lace split and the stretcher gave out entirely. The pilot awoke again and started wailing, crying out "my legs oh god my fucking legs" over and over like a mantra. Erik stood over him, hands on his hips, breathing deeply. Now my brother did not look so optimistic.

I sat down against a tree and took shallow sips of water, barely enough to moisten my cracked lips. Jenna sat down beside me, stared at me with open concern. I nodded, trying to convey confidence, but I was exhausted, and I had no idea what to do now. The pilot kept moaning, begging for death, and I started to wonder if maybe we should grant him his wish. If we did not reach help soon he would die anyway, only slowly and painfully, screaming in agony through the night.

"Erik," I said. "We need to do something."

"I know," said my brother. "I think maybe one of us should go for help, hike down to the car. Drive to the nearest town. I could do it."

"That could take hours," Jenna said. "And it would be dark by the time you came back. How would you find us?"

"Flashlights," Erik said. "The Rangers would have flashlights."

"What is the nearest town from here?" I asked, thinking of our drive up from Jasper. We had driven for at least an hour beyond any semblance of civilization.

"Maybe there's a logging post," Erik said. "Or a fishing camp."

"We'd have a better chance if we carried him," I said. "It would take longer to get to the car, but at least we'd have him with us."

"I'm not sure we can carry him," Jenna said. "He's in too much pain and he's losing blood. He must have internal injuries."

"Oh-ho-ho, god...." The pilot groaned. "Fucking kill me...."

Erik and Jenna and I looked at each other. Erik shook his head.

"He is suffering," I said.

"Sean," Erik said quietly. "We can't just let him die."

"He's in so much pain," Jenna whispered.

Erik paced back and forth, his face worried, his arms taut with veins. "A sleeping bag," he said eventually. "We could carry him in a sleeping bag. Carry him down to the car. The campsite can't be far." He looked around through the trees. Not far away slivers of lake were visible. The sun inched toward the mountains to the west. "I'll be back in a few minutes."

He took off into the woods, leaving Jenna and I to sit beside the pilot.

The sun sank lower on the horizon. Jenna slapped at bugs while I felt the pilot's forehead. It burned with fever. Sweat poured from his scalp, mixing with dried blood and burnt skin. He spoke in slurred tongues, his only recognizable words expressions of pain. Jenna closed her eyes and covered her ears. I put my arm around her and she let me hold her.

"Kill me..." the pilot muttered. "Fucking kill me... kill me...."

Jenna rested her chin on my shoulder and leaned her face toward my ear. "Maybe we should just do it," she whispered, crying softly. Her breath was hot against my face. Her body shook and I held her tighter.

"I think he is going to die," I told her, not sure what else to say. Looking around I saw nothing but trees, and I realized, with a strange sickening feeling, that we had not even checked the plane wreckage for other survivors. There might have been others, backs broken, pinned beneath their seats, burning alive. I tried to shut out the images.

Erik returned sometime later. I had no idea how much time had passed. I felt dizzy and my whole body ached and stung.

"It was farther than I thought," he said. "We're a ways off course."

He had a fresh bottle of water and we all drank. We tried to feed the pilot but he spat it up again, choking. Erik turned his head and the water dribbled from his mouth, roped with blood.

"Erik," I whispered. "He's going to die."

Erik sat down and cradled the pilot's head in his lap. Jenna went over and sat beside Erik, resting her head on his shoulder. He leaned into her, and they looked so natural together I wondered for a moment if I had ever meant anything to her, regardless of what had happened in the tent the previous night. I could see that she loved my brother, loved his gentle spirit, always had. She wanted to protect him from anything that might rattle his optimism. Right then I wanted to rescue the pilot, drag him through the forest, kicking and screaming if necessary, so that he might survive and my brother would not be disappointed.

Wordlessly I unzipped the sleeping bag and began to wrap it around the pilot's feet. He screamed at my touch. He was a big man, late forties probably, stocky, his limbs thick like meat. Erik and Jenna started to help me. The pilot's body was a limp, slack, burned thing, incapable of assisting us in moving itself into the sleeping bag. We could not move his hips and belly, the heaviest part of him, off the ground to get the bag around him.

"It's not fucking working," I said, cursing the pilot in my mind for fighting so hard not to move. Couldn't he see we were trying to help him?

Jenna punched a tree in frustration, sucked back a sob between her clenched teeth. Erik sat back on the ground, winded, sweating, covered in the pilot's blood.

"Kill me," the pilot whispered. "Kill me... kill me."

"How?" Jenna said, and I wasn't sure if she was talking to him or us.

"We can't," Erik said. "We can't kill him. We just have to move. Come on."

He stood up, but we did not follow.

"He wants it," Jenna said, tears dripping from her eyes. "He's suffering, Erik."

"It's wrong," Erik said.

"It's merciful," I said. I wanted to defend Jenna, show her that I could take charge now with what needed to be done.

"It's one thing if he dies on his own," Erik said in a low voice. "But we can't just snuff him out."

"It's cruel to watch him suffer," Jenna said.

"We could go to jail," Erik said. "No one would understand. We pulled him out of a plane, then killed him? What jury would show us mercy?"

"We could say he died of his wounds," I said. "Which he will, if we don't get help soon."

"We saved his life," Erik said. "It would be for nothing if we just killed him."

"Kill me...." The pilot's voice was barely a whisper now. "Please kill me...."

"He's begging for it, Erik," I said.

"He doesn't know what he's saying," said my brother.

"He does know what he's saying," said Jenna. "He's asking for mercy."

Erik stood up and paced around, staring desperately at the forest, as if it might provide some solution he could not think of on his own. But the trees replied only with silence, their hard bark a shield against our pleas for help.

"I won't see either of you go to jail," Erik said. "We just have to carry him until we reach help or he dies."

He bent toward the pilot and gently took hold of the man's shirt, but at the slightest tug the pilot shrieked in pain and lashed out, swatting Erik's arm away. Erik looked up at Jenna, and then at me. He leaned against a tree and rubbed his eyes. He looked totally defeated.

"How would we do it?" he asked. "A gun would be merciful."

"We don't have a gun," I said, wishing we had brought our .22 rifle. We usually brought the gun camping, for protection. We had left it at home this time.

"We could muffle him with the sleeping bag," Jenna said, but she cringed at her own suggestion. "Oh God, I don't think I could handle suffocation."

I looked around for a large rock, but the earth was covered in foliage. Then I felt the hatchet on my belt. I held it up for Erik and Jenna.

"Like an ax murder?" Erik whispered, his hands shaking.

I turned the tool over, hit my palm with the flat end of the blade. He covered his face with his hands. Jenna looked at the hatchet nervously, fresh tears dripping from her eyes.

"Who's going to do it?" she asked.

We sat in silence for a long moment, none of us looking at one another. Erik leaned back against the tree, stared up at the setting sun.

"I should do it," he said, his voice cracking. "I'm the oldest. I should take responsibility."

Jenna crawled over and sat beside him, wrapped her arms around him. He was crying now too, and I felt a knot form in my stomach. The grip of the hatchet was hot in my hand. Jenna gently kissed Erik's cheek. She turned her teary eyes to me.

"I don't think I'm strong enough," she said quietly. "I don't want to do it wrong."

I did not blame her for disqualifying herself, because we both knew I was the one who inevitably had to do it. If she didn't use enough force, either because of exhaustion or hesitation, she would have to hack at the pilot's skull again and again until he was definitively dead. She knew I would not hold back, and we both knew we could not let Erik destroy his entire worldview by crossing a line that could not be re-crossed.

"I'll do it quickly," I said.

Erik looked up at me, almost protested, but did not. I crouched over the pilot. The man was breathing softly now, his chest sputtering like the engine of his plane, air hissing in and out of his mouth in bursts. A thin blood bubble formed on his lips and bobbed with every labored breath.

Suddenly I hated Erik and Jenna for making me do this, for pushing the responsibility on me, even though I knew I was the only one capable of doing what needed to be done. A part of me knew it would be merciful to end the pilot's suffering, cruel to prolong his misery. But now Erik and Jenna could separate themselves from me, unified in their innocence. Jenna would never touch me again, never reach for me in the darkness, out of interest or consolation or anything. I would never have her. She would choose Erik, with his gentle spirit and striving innocence.

"If I do this," I said. "We can never tell anybody. Ever. We tell people that the pilot died of his injuries, despite our efforts to save him. Nobody but us will ever know the truth."

Erik and Jenna looked at each other, then looked at me and nodded. A covenant formed, I had bound them to my sin. My brother could have Jenna, and frankly he deserved it, as he was the innocent one. I was the tough one, the doer of dirty work, the protector of the good. It would be a long hike back to the car, either that night in the darkness, or the next day in the sober light of morning. In either case we three would have plenty of time to think about what we had done. Plenty of years ahead to justify the act, to tell ourselves we had done everything we could to save a life, to wonder if there was anything more we could have done, anything we did not think of. Years to rationalize and reflect and repent, and in our shared resolve to keep the truth a secret, I knew Erik and Jenna would suffer right along with me.

The trees cast long shadows across the darkening forest. I gripped the wooden handle of the hatchet, aimed for the wound in the pilot's forehead, and brought the flat end of the blade down on his skull as hard as I could.

Chapter 9

Odd-Numbered Streets

Nothing good ever came from a call at 4:38 AM. The tinny, irritating blare of his ring-tone bleated off the blue pre-dawn walls of the bedroom. Detective Elton Trumbull groped for the flip-phone and clawed it open.

"Trumbull." Realizing how much his first spoken word of the day sounded like "trouble." "A what-now?"

The dispatcher repeated his stammering news. Trumbull had to sit up to hear the message again.

"Who is this?" he asked with a deep sigh. "No, Bobby, I'm just joshin' ya. I'm on my way."

He clipped his phone shut. Outside the street lights glowed yellow. No sign of dawn.

"Elton," murmured his wife, Sally Anne. "What is it?"

Trumbull stood from the bed and reached for the pair of pants hanging over the bedside chair.

"You don't want to know."

Trumbull stood outside the tenement building, listening to the morning crickets. He sipped the sugary cup of coffee that Pettingill had brought him, thinking about how he had to endure five more years of this job if he wanted to retire with a full pension. In the back of his mind, hovering like a thunder cloud, lurked the recent report from his doctor that his blood pressure was now "approaching the red."

A Toyota sedan pulled up next to the light-flashing patrol cars, and out stepped Detective Ken Brown, the department's junior to Trumbull's senior, looking well-groomed and ready, even at five in the miserable morning, as if he had just stepped away from moonlighting as a model for Brooks Brothers.

"Where's mine?" Brown asked, meaning Trumbull's coffee.

"This is it," Trumbull replied. "I already drank mine."

Together they watched as Pettingill, the photographer, crouched in various angles around the horrid thing that had rousted them all from sleep, snapping off quick shots, pivoting, snapping again.

Nearby, a patrol officer interviewed the witness who had called it in, a harried man in a Dunkin Donuts uniform. Someone had already taped off the scene, and a sick-looking officer was standing guard to make sure nobody used the tenement's front door.

"Shall we?" Brown asked.

Trumbull led the way over to the entranceway. The two of them stared down at the gaping, swollen-eyed, congealed-blood-spattered human head sitting in a thin pool of its own excretions on the front steps of the building. The flashes from Pettingill's camera made the head look instantaneously alive, and peeved.

Pettingill stood up. "Reckon I'm good, Elton. Now I think I'll go back to the office and throw up."

The photographer staggered back to his car.

Trumbull turned to Brown, who was regarding the head with a forced, clinical detachment.

"You don't suppose it just kinda fell off?" Trumbull asked.

"That would be unusual," Brown replied.

A swarm of police officers- Lawson, Georgia's entire P.D., it looked like- were combing the grounds of the tenement, rustling through the bushes. No one had yet discovered a headless corpse.

"The first problem is I.D.," Trumbull said. He crouched by the head and pointed a flashlight at the open mouth. "He wasn't carrying his wallet in his teeth. Reckon it must be in his pants. Which are hopefully still covering his legs."

"The rest of him can't've gotten far," Brown said.

Trumbull noticed the Chief had not yet arrived. The other officers shrugged at one another, as if they were all looking for somebody's missing car keys.

"Could be the head was placed here post-mortem," Brown said, looking around, but not moving. "I'd expect more blood if this is where decapitation took place."

Trumbull felt his stomach flutter, a ripple that eventually reached his heart and settled there. He walked over to where the witness was gripping himself around the arms, like he'd been freshly pulled from a river.

"You the one called it in?" Trumbull asked.

"I goddamn stepped on the thing," the young man stammered. "Don't think I'll ever forget that. Good Lord."

"Do you know the man?"

"No, but I ain't looked real close."

"Mind taking a gander?"

"I ain't goin' over there. I don't know him. I was just goin' to work."

"All right."

"He might be one of them dopers," the man speculated, his fingers nervously plucking at his uniform. "You reckon this is a drug thing?"

The Randle Green Apartments on 9th Avenue were Lawson's narcotics epicenter, the consequences of which brought P.D. to the tenement several times a week.

"That'd be my guess," Trumbull told the young man.

The head was packaged up in a Playmate 5-gallon beverage cooler- which someone thought was both sterile and inconspicuous- and driven by an unlucky rookie straight to the county crime lab in Albany.

Trumbull and Brown spent the morning waking up residents at the Randle Green Apartments and asking them, in delicate terms, if they had seen or heard anything suspicious the previous night. Despite a few snippets detailing the usual chicanery at Randle Green, the overwhelming response from the tenement was N. S. N.

"Nobody saw nothing," Detective Brown said in his best south-of-the-tracks accent. "And nobody seemed to be missing a head."

"If they were missing a head," Trumbull replied. "It's likely they would have seen nothing."

Chief Dobbs arrived and promptly called Albany P.D., to procure reinforcement detectives to assist Trumbull and Brown with the interviews.

"Come on now," Chief Dobbs thundered. "A head doesn't just show up out of nowhere. Somebody must know the young man."

"They don't talk to po-lice down here in the Odds, Chief," Trumbull said.

"They won't talk to you, Ken?" Dobbs asked Detective Brown.

Brown stared back at him with a tired because-I'm-black? expression. "I'm from Macon, sir," Brown said. "These folks don't know me."

Just before noon, a high-pitched wailing arose from somewhere in the tenement. Trumbull and Brown, and everybody else, descended upon an open apartment door, expecting to find a corpse, sans head. Instead they found a young woman pacing in and out of her apartment, crying, waving her hands at anyone who tried to get near.

Officer Katie Pierce was the closest respondent to the woman. "She says her cousin's been missing two days, and now she just got a call on her phone saying he ain't coming back."

"Who called?" asked Detective Brown.

"Haven't found out."

The police gathered around in silence as the woman's hysteria eventually down-swirled to a whimper. Detective Trumbull stepped forward.

"Ma'am," he said. "Do you have a photo of your cousin?"

Without really answering his question the woman began sifting through piles in the mess of her apartment, before eventually remembering that she had a picture of her cousin on her phone. She showed a phone pic to Trumbull and Brown of a young black man in a do-rag, grinning and smoking a thin cigar. Trumbull and Brown exchanged the Glance of Certainty.

Officer Pierce stepped forward to comfort the young woman as a fresh wave of sobbing poured forth. Trumbull and Brown shooed the other officers away, and waited patiently to interview their new witness.

"N. S. N.," Brown said, as they stood outside by their cars. "Her own flesh and blood, and she wouldn't even say he was dealing drugs."

"At least now we know who he is," said Trumbull. "Or was." Headquarters had just texted them the file on one Antoine Grimes, age 20, frequent local arrestee on charges of drug possession, assault, and public intoxication. The challenge now, Trumbull lamented, would be to find someone in the building willing to spill on who Grimes might have been beefing with.

"Y'know, I grew up on the south side, in a building just like this one," said Detective Brown. "When I was young, crack was first coming through, and those were bad times. Twenty-five years later, we still got this nonsense."

"Well, Lawson is a trafficking stop," said Trumbull. "It all goes up to Atlanta, and from there...." He made a limp, sweeping gesture to indicate the rest of the world. "In my day you didn't even smell marijuana, and if you did, the church ladies raised hell."

"I would never arrest someone for reefer. Too much paperwork."

"I did. Had to. I'll tell ya, though...." He shook his head, found himself checking his radial pulse, which had become a recent habit. "I'd grow grass for everyone myself if it got them to give up these other things."

"This is some Mexican shit here," said Detective Brown. "They cut off heads and who-knows-what. It's war down there."

Trumbull said nothing. Across the parking lot Chief Dobbs was standing by the tenement entranceway with a few uniformed officers, talking to the local TV news crew.

"Now it'll be on the six o'clock news," Brown said. "We better get someone to talk before all the nuts spill out the jar."

"In all these years I've never understood why people won't talk to po-lice," Trumbull said. "I mean, I know why: they're scared, repercussions and whatnot. But a man gets his head cut off...."

A second news van arrived, and the reporter rushed over to Chief Dobbs.

"What do you suppose people think when they see something like this on the news?" Trumbull asked.

"You know they film that zombie show about an hour from here," said Brown. "Everyone watches it. People probably see a severed head staring up at 'em, they think there's a camera nearby."

"...we're investigating the possibility of a drug connection, at this time," Chief Dobbs was telling the news cameras. "This type of crime might be- might be one drug organization sending a message...."

"And that message is: we're completely fucked," Brown muttered.

Trumbull had no argument.

"We better get to those interviews," Brown said.

"I need to get home for lunch," Trumbull said. He wasn't particularly hungry, but seeing his wife always evened out his pulse. "Why don't you come get lunch, Ken?"

"All right," Brown said.

Trumbull had silenced his phone, and he felt it vibrate in his pocket.

"Hold it," he said to Brown. He answered his phone. It was Bobby at dispatch again. "Now I'm starting to think you're joshin' me, Bob," Trumbull said, after Bobby gave him the latest news. "Yeah, we'll head on over."

He hung up. So there would be no visit home for lunch.

"Body?" Brown asked.

Trumbull shook his head. It was getting to be a hot day. "They found a leg," he said.

Brown nodded. "Just one?"

The severed leg was found next to a dumpster, out behind the Lawson KFC on 7th Ave, by a counter clerk who had drawn the short straw of taking out the garbage. It was the leg of a youngish black man, and the detectives agreed that it must have lately belonged to Antoine Grimes, unless, God be merciful, there was more than one former citizen of Lawson, GA currently separated into pieces.

"I'm not in the mood for a goshdarn scavenger hunt," Trumbull griped.

Pettingill, green-faced, photographed the leg, while the same unsmiled-upon rookie from head duty returned to Family Dollar for another Playmate cooler.

"Here's a question," Brown said. "Let's say parts of Mr. Grimes turn up all over the county; shouldn't the town with the most body by cumulative weight take the case?"

Trumbull glared at his partner.

"Let's pray they find the torso in Wilmington," Brown continued.

"You heard the chief," Trumbull said. "High-profile case. It's on us, and we need to goshdarn solve it. No sleep or family time till we do."

"Shit, I'm missing my son's whole childhood," Brown muttered.

Trumbull thought of his own kids, grown and off at college. How much of their lives had he spent sifting through the sewage of the drug war? When he'd first joined the force, policing was about making sure no drunks caused trouble on Friday nights.

A call came in from dispatch, stating that a person claiming to be the girlfriend of Antoine Grimes had called in to report threatening phone calls, and the detectives determined that this might be what the old dime novels referred to as "a lead." They left Pettingill and a patrol officer to deal with the severed leg, and drove to 15th Ave, where lived Michaela Watkins, whom both men were praying would be cooperative.

"You don't know nothin'," Detective Brown squawked, throwing Michaela Watkins' words back into her quivering face. "Antoine ran with a drug crew. That ain't no secret. Who they beefin' with?"

"I dunno," Michaela repeated.

"Ma'am, at this time we're not looking to link any associates to any criminal activity," said Trumbull.

"Huh?" said Michaela Watkins.

"We just want to find the guys who killed Antoine. You don't have to snitch on anyone."

The apartment smelled of fast-food, used diapers, and the overflowing bags of garbage in the kitchen. Festering dishes lay discarded on the counters. A dozen fans sat perched at various location, sputtering a dozen different rhythms of malfunction. Still the apartment was murderously hot.

"This is some Mexican intimidation shit," said Detective Brown. "You seen any Mexicans around, Miss Watkins, maybe slingin' dope, like Antoine?"

"I don't know no Mexicans."

"What about Antoine's boys? He get in any arguments lately?"

"I don't know nothin' 'bout that."

"You said you received a threatening phone call?" Trumbull asked. "What did the caller say?"

Michaela rubbed her hands on her bulging denim thighs. "I think it was a wrong number," she said finally.

"Come on now, what'd they say?" Brown asked, his temper rising with his inflection.

"I ain't heard."

"You recognize the number?" Trumbull asked.

"Nope."

Brown: "What. Did. They. Say?"

Michaela rubbed her thighs again. She fumbled a bent cigarette out of a pack in her pocket table, and lit it. "They say Antoine ain't gon' say shit now, and I better not neither."

"Man or woman on the phone?" Trumbull asked.

"Man. I guess."

"Antoine ain't gon' say shit about what?" asked Brown.

"I dunno."

"Miss Watkins, I think you do know."

"You aren't in any trouble, ma'am," Trumbull offered.

"I don't know nothin' 'bout that," the woman said.

"All right, listen," Trumbull said, pacing in the sweltering kitchen. "Something terrible happened to Antoine. Something ungodly. We have a decent Georgia community here, Miss Watkins, and we're trying to preserve that decency. We can't have what happened to Antoine happen to people. You have to help us. It doesn't make you a snitch. But I can't- we can't-"

His mouth was dry, and his breathing tightened. He wanted to ask for a glass of water, but the state of the dishware in the Watkins kitchen made him hesitate. His pulse ticked upwards. He gripped his wrist and closed his eyes. He had not eaten anything since his hurried breakfast of toast and a banana. Outside the air was so thick even the crickets had given up chirping.

Michaela Watkins stared wide-eyed at absolutely nothing, puffing out purple clouds of smoke.

"Ma'am, we're gonna need to get that number off your cell phone," Brown said eventually.

By day's end there were a hundred leads, none of them promising. Another leg had turned up on the outskirts of town, and someone had called in to report what they thought was a dead human body, which turned out to be a dead dog. Nobody had seen anything, and nobody knew anything. At 2 AM Trumbull and Brown headed back to their respective homes to catch a few fitful hours of sleep.

Sally Anne awoke when Trumbull bulled his way into the bedroom. Thirty years as a police wife, and she still woke up to greet him when he came in late. Trumbull was grateful for that.

"Sally, I don't know what-all I seen and heard today," Trumbull said, sitting on the edge of the bed in his boxer shorts and tank top. "I just do not know."

"I saw it on the news," his wife said. "Can't think of what to say."

"What is there to say? There's no rules anymore." He climbed into bed. "We still haven't found the body. Or, y'know, the torso." The word "torso" sounded vile to him.

"It's a drug thing, I gather," said Sally Anne.

"I just don't understand drugs," Trumbull said. "Why would someone want to lose their mind? On purpose?"

"Not everyone wants to," said Sally Anne, resting a hand on his shoulder.

"Everyone south of Main Street," Trumbull said.

"I don't know what to tell ya, Bud," Sally Anne said. "There's problems out there we can't solve, and the Church can't either. In my opinion, a man your age oughtn't be staggering in at two in the morning. He should be watching the game shows with his wife, playing Backgammon."

"I can't argue with you, Sally-"

Trumbull's cell phone rang.

"Dang it now."

Sally Anne sighed and lay back against her pillow.

Trumbull thumbed open his phone. "Trumbull's body shop."

There was silence on the other end of the line.

"I'm just joshin', Bobby, what is it?"

Trumbull and Brown arrived at an abandoned wood frame house on East 37th Ave, the last southern street in Lawson before the town gave way to swamp. A patrol car idled by the sidewalk, lights flashing. The young officer stood nervously in the dirt driveway, a flashlight shaking in his hand.

Trumbull's standard outfit for a middle-of-the-night call was jeans and a plaid shirt, but he noticed that Brown was wearing a suit, a different one now, perhaps because it was technically a new day.

"Man out walking his dog, called it in," said the patrol officer.

Trumbull turned on his own flashlight.

"Where is it?"

"I don't know," said the patrol officer. "The man just called in a blood trail."

"Walking his dog at two-thirty AM?" Brown scoffed.

"It's cooler at night," the officer speculated.

Trumbull and Brown directed their flashlight beams down at the tall amber grass growing outside the vacant house. A thick smear of dried blood led in a sloshy trail toward the house, vanishing under the black, toothless maw of a rotted porch. The detectives followed the trail to the porch, stepping carefully, scanning the grass for evidence. The smell emanating from under the porch could only have been one thing.

"Well, Ken," Trumbull said. "I've got high blood pressure, and I ain't crawlin' under there."

Brown hesitated, stepping lightly from one foot to the other like a boy at a junior high dance. "I'm sorry, Elton," he said, running his fingers over the fine fabric of his suit coat. "These threads cost me all of last month's overtime. It's Armani. From Italy."

"It's the middle of the night, Ken. Nobody but the ghosts can see you in that suit."

"Dress the part, act the part."

"You could get a pair of sweatpants and a Falcons tee-shirt over at Sears without hardly dipping into your retirement."

Detective Brown knelt beside the porch. "I'll write the report," he said. "Whatever we find, whatever shit-hell rabbit hole it takes us down, I'll type it up, and you can go home and get some sleep."

"You insubordinate son of a gun."

They agreed that Brown would handle report-writing for the entirety of the case, before Trumbull got down on his belly and wormed his way into the filthy chasm beneath the porch. He kept the flashlight beam pointed directly ahead of him, at a mysterious lump, avoiding visual contact with whatever other ghastly unspeakables might be living or dead under the porch. At what point, he wondered, had the chain of command broken down? At what sinister juncture had society pitched respect for its elders out the window of a speeding car? A man approaching sixty should not be crawling through grime- and furthermore, his wife would destroy him for destroying his clothes. Right now Sally Anne's proffered game shows and Backgammon had never sounded better.

The smell of the corpse was so vile it cleared Trumbull's head of all thought. He stuffed his shirt collar into his mouth, sucked in a deep breath of air from his own armpit, and groped at the body with his free hand. His palm landed in a sticky sludge of goo.

"You're a rotten apple, Ken!" he called out.

"What's that, Elton?"

The corpse faced away from him. Which is to say, there appeared to be a head, and it seemed to be turned away. Taking another deep breath from within his own shirt,

Trumbull grabbed a sticky fistful of the body's clothing and yanked to turn the thing over. The weight of the torso shifted, and a head thudded against the black dirt. Streams of caked blood smeared the pale face.

Suppressing vomit, Trumbull wriggled out from beneath the porch, army-crawling the way he'd been taught in boot camp almost forty years before. He smeared the blood and viscera from the corpse on his shirt, deciding that tonight's outfit had served its last tour of duty.

Detective Brown helped Trumbull to his feet. Trumbull breathed in a long swallow of cool, damp air.

"Is it our man?" Brown asked.

"There's a body under there," Trumbull said.

"Missing a head?"

"Nope. The usual kind."

"Aw, shit," Brown said.

A year later Trumbull's blood pressure had returned to "a respectable level," according to his doctor. Trumbull spent his days working a security desk at Fulton Plastics in Albany. He spent his nights watching the game shows with his wife.

The desk job was boring and routine and entirely predictable, and came at the expense of a good chunk of what would have been a nice police pension. But he worked the first shift, and he was home every day by four PM, early enough to help Sally Anne start dinner.

He was six months into the job when he received his first trainee, a young man named Brice. Trumbull spent all of an hour orienting Brice on the simple equipment at the security desk, then took him on a walking tour of the plastics plant.

"I make my rounds twice an hour," Trumbull explained. "Breaks up the sittin' a bit."

"You ever get anyone trying to break in?" Brice asked. "Any punks stealing shit?"

"I saw a raccoon last month," said Trumbull. "Couldn't speak to his motives."

"How come they don't let us carry?" Brice asked. "I got my license."

Trumbull shook his head. Here was another gladiator who should have joined the army.

"Maybe when the raccoons start carrying, we will," he said.

"Maybe they'll let me bring my Glock," said Brice. "It's a crazy fuckin' world."

"I know it is."

"You said you been working here six months," Brice said. "What'd you do before this?"

"I was a police detective in Lawson," Trumbull said.

"You retire?"

"Quit early. That crazy world you mentioned got to be too much."

"Shit," Brice said, a new layer of respect coating his tone. "What's the craziest thing you saw while you were a police?"

Trumbull sighed. It had all congealed together, a mass of filth floating in a sewer. "Found a human head on a doorstep last year," he said. That particular piece of refuse would always float to the surface.

"I remember that!" Brice cried. "That was nuts! Like zombie-apocalypse-shit! Why'd they do it?"

"Why'd who do what?"

"Why'd they cut off that guy's head? Was it a drug thing?"

Trumbull stared at his feet as they walked. Only ten more years, and he could retire from this job too. "I don't know," he said. "We never caught the guys who did it."

Chapter 10

Saucy Jack

Laura did not cry at her sister's funeral. Janet had been eight years older than her, the first-born, tall, quiet, a loner. Laura was short, dark-featured, brooding, and from the time she was a child always felt she was a thorn in her sister's heel.

Emily cried- copious, middle-child tears. Emily was the one who reached out to others, pulled them close, made them do and be what she wanted. Countless times she had tried to make an intimate out of Laura, their age difference being a more-relatable three years, but Laura resisted. Laura loved her sisters. They were her blood. But they had never been her friends.

Janet had been killed in a car accident while driving to Vermont with her husband for a ski holiday. Hank was currently in a coma, with two broken legs, his jaw wired shut, his right arm shattered. Mercifully, Laura thought, Janet and Hank had no children.

Sitting alone at the back of the church, Laura stoically tuned out Uncle Mason's eulogy. She reflected that she had never really known Janet, nor Hank, which she regretted, but not enough to bring her to tears.

A few days after the funeral Emily stopped by Laura's condo with Chinese take-out and a bottle of wine. Laura had been reading when the doorbell rang.

"I just can't believe it, she was always such a careful driver," Emily sobbed when they were deep into the wine. "She never had a single accident. Not even as a teenager. You remember how she used to drive us everywhere?"

"Vaguely," Laura replied.

"Apparently it wasn't her fault," Emily said. "The breaks gave out, or something. And they were on a steep slope. What a disaster. And poor Hank."

Emily broke down in fresh tears. Laura frowned and considered. Yes, poor Hank. But Hank Who? Janet had married Hank after knowing him only six months. Hank had been married once before, Laura knew. Beyond that she knew almost nothing about him, not where he was from originally, nothing about his family. They had spoken maybe three times, including once at Janet's wedding.

"I think she was a very lonely person," Emily lamented. "She lived so long without any real love in her life. Then Hank came along. Then-" She snapped her fingers with chilling finality.

Laura did not know what to say.

"I worry about you too, Laur," Emily said. "You don't have anyone either."

"So what," Laura said.

"Both of my sisters, such solitary people. Were you guys not happy growing up? Are you not happy now?"

"I'm perfectly content," Laura said, which was predominantly true. She was thirty-four, and had accepted the notion that she would never be a plucky, kid-carting wife and mother, like Emily. Nor was she a career girl, chasing the delusion of a corner office and a luxury SUV. She was devoted to her one true passion, reading. She was a collector and lover of books, all subjects, all genres. In reading Laura felt normal. Curled up on her couch, hot chocolate turning lukewarm in the mug beside her, Hudson Bay blanket draped over her knees, she felt totally at peace.

"I don't know how you can be content," Emily said. She was half-smiling, and Laura saw she was not trying to pick a fight. "Look at your life. All you do is read. You go to work, at the *library*, surrounded by books. You come home, more books. Shades drawn. No light, no people, no conversation."

"That's very elegiac, Em."

"Very what?"

"Elegiac."

"When was the last time you had a boyfriend?"

"Please, Mom, I'm not in the mood for this one."

"When was the last time you went on a date? Went to a party?"

"I don't know."

"You need people in your life, Laura. I don't want to see you end up like Janet."

Laura almost asked if that meant she would one day die in a car accident with a strange man she had married in desperation.

"I have a favor to ask you," Emily said, refilling Laura's glass.

Laura squinted suspiciously at the wine. "What?"

"Someone needs to take care of Jack," Emily said. "Now that Janet's gone. We don't know what will happen with Hank. I think you should take him. I think it would do you good to have a new friend, someone to care for. It would show you how important companionship is."

Laura stared at her. "Who is Jack?"

"Janet's parrot."

"The bird?" Laura straightened up, instantly sober and alert. "You want me to take the bird? That squawking thing?"

"He needs a home, Laur. Charlie and I can't take him because we already have cats, and we work all the time, and he bothers Peyton and Mackenzie with his screeching, and-"

"He bothers *me* with his screeching," Laura objected. She had entirely forgotten about Jack, Janet's blue and gold macaw parrot, whom Janet had adopted at some point during her eternal spinsterhood. Laura had only seen Jack a handful of times. The parrot was a screeching, bobbing, wall-eyed, beautiful but useless thing, and she could not fathom, in the deepest crevice of her mind, why anyone would ever keep a bird as a pet.

"Emily, look at me," Laura said, suddenly feeling exhausted. "Do I look the kind of person who could take care of a jungle bird?"

Emily's face brightened, as if she had been waiting for this very question. "You had that pet rat in college. What was his name? Jonathan? He had only one eye?"

"Jonas," Laura said. Old Jonas, the poor, tormented creature she had adopted from the behavioral science lab at Cornell. Jonas the rat had been born with a disfigured stump for a left forearm, a mutation which made him the pariah of the pack. The other rats had tortured him mercilessly. He had been in so many fights that his ears were bitten and scarred, and one of his eyes had been scratched out. But Jonas had been intelligent, a master of the mazes and other tests the behaviorists had put him through, and he had the gentle heart of a pacifist, despite his myriad beatings.

For a moment Laura missed Jonas intensely. He had lived to be four years old, and she had cried when she awoke one morning to find his rock-solid corpse squatting in the corner of his tank. Suddenly she knew she would give in to her sister's request. Emily, who remembered everything, had unearthed and exploited Laura's one long-buried, sentimental weakness.

"What would I have to do?" Laura asked.

"Feed him, play with him, talk to him. He can talk. He lost his companion, and he needs someone to look after him."

Laura detested the saccharine, Christian-Children's-Fund pitch in Emily's voice, resented even more the bald relief her sister exuded now that the bird would not become her own burden.

"There's one more thing," Emily said. "Jack was with them in the car. He broke his wing. The doctors say he may never fly again."

Laura felt exhausted. Two hours ago she had been relaxing with Ann Rule's latest true-crime thriller, a story of marital discord gone deliciously wrong, drinking up every scandalous page. How had her quiet evening come to this?

Laura installed Jack's sizable cage in the corner of her living room, instantly realizing how small her condo was. The book shelves lining every wall confined the space even more. She set up Jack's cage near the window because she thought the view would stimulate him. This worked for about two hours, until a squirrel flitted past outside, and Jack's screech sent a bolt of adrenalin through Laura's heart. She moved the cage to the dining room nook, dragged the dinner table out into the living room, into her reading space. The new angle of her reading couch filled her with profound unease. The light was different. Her home had been invaded and disrupted.

She filled Jack's food dish and water bottle, but had no idea when or how much he was supposed to eat. He just sat there on his perch, bobbing sometimes, turning away from her whenever she took a step toward him. The bowl of seeds and nuts remained untouched for several hours. Laura gave up, went to work, came back and found her condo smelled of bird shit.

When she awoke the next day and inspected Jack's food dish, there seemed to be a dent in the pile. There was also food stuff littered across the bottom of the cage.

"Well, did you eat or not?" Laura whispered.

Jack cocked his head at her. She stared at the cast and sling on his arm, thought it must be uncomfortable. Good, she thought, now he knows how I feel.

She went into her bedroom and tried to read. Reading in bed was usually something she did at night, before she fell asleep. Most of her serious reading took place in the living room, where she could look up and see her hundreds of books, decorating her wooden shelves like trophies. Laura read broadly and thoroughly. Once she found an author, she read their entire catalogue. She read high-brow literature, supermarket mysteries, graduate-level textbooks. Her special love was true crime, real-life stories of murder and mayhem, the dirty laundry of America's cotton-white middle class. Corruption, scandal, affairs, jealousies, financial ruin, sociopaths dreaming of better lives without their partners, poisoning each other for the family fortune. Laura delighted in the cavities rotting beneath America's pearly whites. But what she liked most about the books was that the murderers were almost invariably caught, tripped up by their own arrogance, their lack of foresight, or forensic evidence. Laura had never told this to anyone, but she felt an incomparable rush when she read about a murderer receiving his comeuppance. The punishment of the guilty filled her with a deep sense of satisfaction.

Laura's library had been her lair, her retreat, her sanctuary.

Until Jack arrived. The bird screeched at her whenever she entered the room, his vocal canon high-pitched and throaty. For the first three days Laura felt like a jungle soldier trying to creep out of sight of a sniper, slinking around her own house, her heart shocked by the sudden and unpredictable screams of the macaw. On the fourth morning Jack shrieked just as Laura took a bite of her oatmeal, and she dropped her clattering spoon to the floor.

"Jesus Christ, give me a break!" she hollered. The parrot bobbed on his perch, tapped his water bottle with his beak. Laura strode across the room, peered into his cage. He turned away from her, but she stared at the water bottle. "Are you drinking, or what?" she asked. "Don't you ever get thirsty?"

"*Get me a drink!*" the parrot said, his voice so high and startlingly clear that Laura did a double take.

"I don't know if he's eating or drinking," Laura told the veterinarian when she brought Jack in for a check-up for his broken wing. "I think he is. How much do they eat?"

"You should give him fresh food every day," the vet replied, inspecting Jack's broken wing. The bird sat motionless on his perch, head turned away.

"I bought him a mix at the pet store," Laura said. "He only seems to eat the sunflower seeds though."

"That's not uncommon. He may pick out his favorites and just eat those."

"He's not even my pet," Laura said, not sure why she said this, but feeling she should justify her ignorance. "I'm just watching him. For my sister."

The vet nodded, continued to examine Jack.

"He screeches every time I come in the room," Laura said. "Is that going to stop? Once he recognizes me?"

"He probably screeches *because* he recognizes you," said the doctor. "It's his way of saying hello."

"Sometimes he screeches for no reason."

"That can happen too."

Not the answer Laura hoped for. "Why is he turning his head away like that?"

"Well, it may be because of his wing. He may be ashamed of his injury, or the sling, and he doesn't want you to see him in a state of weakness. Just like we humans might do, when we have a cut or a bruise. Birds have a highly-developed sense of self-preservation."

Laura frowned at Jack, unconvinced. She wanted to tell the vet that the bird had a brain the size of a dried fig, and thus did not have a highly-developed sense of anything.

"He may also not be comfortable around you yet," the vet speculated. "You said he belongs to your sister?"

"Belonged, actually. She's deceased."

"Oh, yes," said the vet, and Laura realized he probably knew this. "I'm so sorry." He cleared his throat and continued his analysis. "Macaws mate for life. Jack may have chosen your sister as his mate, and so, when he sees you, he sees a stranger, or maybe even an intruder."

"*He* sees an intruder? *He's* the intruder. In *my* home."

The doctor finished his examination of Jack, leaned back against the counter and crossed his arms. "Macaws should only be kept as pets by people who are serious about the commitment. They're social creatures and they require attention. Many new bird owners are not prepared for the longevity of the relationship."

"How long do they live?" Laura asked.

"A healthy macaw can live seventy-five, eighty years. Or longer."

"Eighty years!?"

"So you should think about the commitment," the vet said. "A parrot is not like a goldfish. In the meantime, socialize with Jack. Open the door to his cage. Talk to him. Build trust. If he decides to bond with you, I can promise you you will both develop a deeply rewarding relationship."

Laura was horrified. She stared at Jack, who was watching her with one all-encompassing eye, studying her as if to say: "Hey, bitch, I didn't ask for this either."

"Now, I'm going to send you home with Jack's medications," the vet continued. "You'll have to administer them with this. Don't worry, I'll show you how to use it." He produced a plastic plunger.

"They can live eighty years!" Laura cried into her phone. "I'm thirty-four! The fucker could outlive me!"

"Well, I suppose you could put him up for adoption," Emily said, sounding hurt. "He should stay with someone at least until his wing heals, though."

Laura collapsed onto her couch. Jack bobbed in his cage, pecking at the rubber mouse toy she had bought him.

"I can't do this," she told her sister.

"I think you can do this," Emily replied. "You took care of that *rat*." Laura could almost hear the shudder in her voice. "I'd be disappointed if you gave up already," Emily added. "This is a very difficult time for all of us, and we haven't asked you for much, Laura."

This was true. Laura had not helped plan Janet's funeral. Neither had she helped her mother and Emily with any posthumous business, going through Janet's old house, cataloging and sorting her possessions. Laura had not even been to see Hank at the hospital, even though he had reportedly come out of his coma, and was now lying in bed in the ICU. Taking the bird was a small sacrifice, and Laura felt selfish for not contributing more. She hung up with Emily, resolved to make an effort to accommodate Jack.

"So what do you want for dinner, you big, blue dummy?" she asked the bird, contemplating whether to make herself pasta for one, or chicken cordon bleu, for one. She said this teasingly. In truth she had quickly grown to love the bird's plumage. His brilliant gold belly, emerald head and sky-blue wings easily made him the most beautiful sight in her condo.

"I guess I'm going to have chicken," she said. "And wine. Lots of wine. Hopefully when I'm drunk I'll be able to give you your medicine, and I won't feel your claws, you ungrateful bastard."

Holding Jack still and sticking the plastic plunger down his throat was unquestionably the most difficult task she had ever attempted. Made no easier by the fact that he shook and scratched her and spat up almost every drop.

"*Get me a drink*," the bird squawked. Laura turned to face him, could not help grinning. His cage door was open and he bobbed leisurely on his perch.

"How 'bout a highball, slick?"

"*Get me a drink.*"

"Yeah, I heard you."

Reading with Jack around was no less difficult. Laura opened his cage and sat down on the couch. She turned on the gas fireplace and delved into the first chapter of her latest thriller. Suddenly Jack shrieked right beside her. Leaping up, she found him awkwardly flapping his one good wing, dancing back and forth on the couch. Jack stared at her aghast, as if her sudden movement had somehow offended him.

"Jack, you little shit, you scared me!" Laura said, her heartbeat throbbing. She watched the bird, saw a strange, predatory look in his eye, his wings upraised. "It's okay," she said. "It's okay, see? I'm sitting back down."

Carefully she sat down and Jack crab-walked to the far end of the couch.

"That's good," she said. "You stay there, and I'll stay here."

Nerves settling back into place, she resumed reading. Jack groomed his good wing, screeching occasionally.

"*Get me a drink.*"

"Whatever you say," Laura told him.

"*Get me a drink!*"

"Jack, *please.*"

"*Oh, Ronnie. Oh! Oh, Ronnie!*"

Laura burst out laughing. "What did you say?"

Jack stared at her, bobbing enthusiastically.

"Oh, Ronnie, what?"

"*Oh, Ronnie. Oh! Oh, Ronnie!*"

She laughed again. Jack looked and sounded like a lover crying out his partner's name in bed. The idea made her blush. It had been longer than she cared to admit since she had last slept with a man. So was the stupid parrot mocking her? Could it see the loneliness deep in the core of her soul? Or did it think it was getting laid?

"He talks," Laura said in one of her increasingly-frequent phone calls to Emily.

"What does he say?" Emily replied. "Polly want a cracker?"

"No crackers. He wants a drink."

"A drink?"

"'Get me a drink! Get me a drink!' That's what he screeches all day long."

"Is he thirsty?"

"At first I thought it might be a signal," Laura said. "Like he was out of water, or something. I checked his bottle a hundred times. It works, and I keep it full."

"Well, Laur, I don't know. Maybe he's an alcoholic."

"He sounds like our old vice principal from middle school. Remember? Mr. Dettweiler? High, squeaky voice." She laughed. "'Get to class, kids! Get to class!'"

"I'm glad you're starting to like him."

"I'm not starting to like him, he's a pain in my ass. He is kind of funny though." She paused, changing her phone to the other ear. "He says something else too."

"Oh yeah?"

Laura scrunched up her throat for her best parrot voice. "'Oh, Ronnie. Oh! Oh, Ronnie!'"

"Umm... that sounds like you're...."

"Having an orgasm?" Laura flushed. She was not sure she had ever used the word "orgasm" with her sister. "That's what he says. 'Oh, Ronnie! Oh, Ronnie!' I swear to god."

"What does it mean when he says that?" Emily asked.

"I have no idea. Maybe he had a parrot girlfriend named Ronnie, back in the jungle."

"Ronnie, Ronnie," Emily said, sounding out the name to herself. "Not Ronnie Mellman?"

"Who?"

"Nothing. I was just thinking... since he was Janet's bird."

"What are you talking about?"

"Her friend, Ronnie Mellman. Did you ever meet him? They worked together."

"No," Laura said. She turned in her living room and narrowed her eyes at Jack, who was watching her closely, his cage door open.

Emily laughed uncomfortably on the other end of the line. "You don't think Janet...."

"Had an affair?" That was exactly what Laura was thinking. It was the kind of sleazy intrigue she read about every day. She worried sometimes that her immersion in true crime sagas tainted her view of the world, or maybe just her view of people.

"She doesn't seem like the type," Emily said. "*Didn't seem.*"

But there was no type, Laura knew. Everybody had affairs. Sordid, sneaky little trysts in upstairs guest rooms when the spouse was out of town. There were no innocent coworker glances in this bloodletting world.

"Maybe she did," Laura said, and to her surprise, the feeling she felt wasn't curiosity but jealousy. Maybe her older sister, the spinster, the pretty but luckless loner, had all sorts of sexual partners nobody in the family knew about. Maybe Janet's well ran deep, while Laura's was conspicuously, transparently shallow.

She decided not to speculate on Janet's love life. Who knows where the parrot had learned the sweaty, sheet-clenching goods about "Ronnie?" She still could not figure out why he always seemed to want a drink. Maybe there was no logic to Jack's communication. Maybe he picked things up from TV.

"Listen," Emily said. "We're going to visit Hank tomorrow. Charlie and I. There's a lot to be done regarding his care and insurance, and we can't track down any of his relatives. If he even has any. I really don't know. But you could come along, Laura. We could use your help."

Laura knew she should agree, even though family errands, whatever the nature, did not interest her at all. "Fine," she said. "Hey, I'll bring the bird. Maybe it will cheer Hank up."

Sounds and images flitted through Hank's consciousness. Waking was now an exercise in confusion, as he tried to remember who he was, where he was, and, less tangibly, what had happened to him. Day by day, though, he was growing stronger. He could flex his left hand, move the fingers to accomplish small goals, like tugging on his sheet or his pillow. He still could not talk- his jaws were wired shut. His legs throbbed with pain. The doctor had told him he would probably walk again, but it would be many months.

He pressed the little blue button on his infusion pump, waited for the warm quilt of morphine to wrap around him. The machine beeped, letting him know it was too soon for his next dose. He would have killed for a scotch, but the morphine drip wasn't bad.

The in-laws were back. Relentless, they were. Emily squeezing his hand, telling him they would take care of everything. Charlie, her husband, pacing the little room. Hank knew how he felt. Wanted to get the hell out of there. Wished he could talk. Emily asked him questions about his health insurance. He knew the answers. Couldn't communicate them. Couldn't even write. Right arm crushed between his body and the door of the car.

He did not remember the accident, only knew the extent of his injuries from the constant reminders from the doctors. Thirty-six broken bones. The one in his ear hurt the most.

Another woman moved around the room. He recognized her vaguely. Short, dark-haired. Janet's other sister. Laura. An odd one.

"Get me a drink."

Hank's heart froze. His glazed eyes scanned the room for the squawking menace. He saw it, bobbing in its cage, blue and gold little fucker. What was it doing here? It was supposed to be dead. Janet had brought it along like he knew she would, and now it was back somehow, haunting him.

"Jack, say hello to Hank."

Hank pressed his little blue button, heard the beep, pressed it again. Sweat broke out on his neck, at the back of his head, inside his itching casts. The bird screeched again, flapped its wings. He shut his eyes and tried to wish the demon back to hell.

The infusion pump for Hank's morphine gave Laura an idea. She had always been a good engineer, a real jerry-rigger, her father had said. She had once made a revolving conveyor for her closet with all her outfits hanging from it. It operated from a foot pedal on the closet floor, so that she could survey her clothes as they passed by, like in a dry cleaner. Now she was fixated on Jack's watering apparatus, curious to see if she could quench the bird's seemingly incessant thirst, maybe get him to shut up about his drink.

She found a used electric analgesia infusing pump online for about sixty bucks. She thought it would be funny if Jack could learn to press a button with his beak, or his talon, to release a shot of water every time he wanted a drink. Constructing the water flow system was not overly difficult. She connected the pump to Jack's water bottle, tweaked the restrictor valve to let about two ounces of water out of the pump every time the button was pressed. The water collected in a little plastic dish. The only difficulty was mounting the hand-control on the wall of Jack's cage in such a way that the device's wires were kept outside the cage. Laura worried that Jack might chew through them and electrocute himself. She sprayed some Grannick's Bitter Apple on the wires to dissuade him.

When the pump and the flow controller were in place, she pressed the button, testing the new feeding mechanism. A trickle of water collected in the plastic dish. Jack sat on the arm of the couch, watching her.

"Oh, yeah," she said, grinning to herself.

"*Oh, Ronnie. Oh! Oh, Ronnie!*"

"Oh, yeah, Ronnie, we're in business."

Building the device, however, was the easy part. Training Jack to use the pump would be the real challenge. She had no idea if he would even understand what it was.

In college Laura had trained Jonas the rat to play "Mary Had a Little Lamb" on her roommate's keyboard. This feat of wonder had been a brief internet sensation. The trick had taken her months, enacted in many stages. She had begun with the fundamental understanding that you train animals to do tricks by using treats. She knew from experiments at the behavioral science lab that Jonas enjoyed a sugar gel solution administered through an eye-dropper. So she started pointing to certain keys on the keyboard with the eye dropper, and when Jonas touched the key with his one good forepaw, she dabbed the key with a little drop of sugar, which he eagerly lapped up. Over time she trained him to touch the keys without the sugar. Using the dropper as a guide, she was able to get him to touch the relevant keys in sequence to produce a slow, elongated rendition of the children's song. When Jonas had come as close to playing "Mary Had a Little Lamb" as she thought him ever likely to get, she filmed the experiment, posted it online, and watched with quiet glee as the video went viral.

Using the same theory of behavioral reward, Laura began training Jack to press the little blue button that would finally get him that elusive drink. Instead of using a dropper with sugar, which she thought he would confuse for his hated plastic medicinal plunger, she rewarded him with sunflower seeds from her own hand. Jack's intelligence surprised her. Once she introduced the device into his cage, he quickly found the button, chomping it with his beak, sometimes producing a trickle of water. Every time the water dribbled out of the infusion pump, Laura fed Jack a sunflower seed.

"*Get me a drink,*" Jack said, bobbing his head as he watched her holding the seed bag.

"Get it yourself."

Over time Jack learned to press the button until the plastic dish was overflowing, because he knew it would earn him more seeds.

"You have to see this," Laura told Emily over the phone. "He doesn't seem to understand that the water is for drinking, but he'll get it eventually."

"I knew you would be good at this," Emily said. "Admit it, Laura, you like the bird."

"All right," Laura said. "I like the bird. Sort of."

"*Oh, Ronnie. Oh! Oh, Ronnie!*"

"Did you hear that?" Laura asked.

"I heard it."

"He's bobbing his head. Whatever it is about Ronnie, he loves it." She winked at the macaw. "Saucy Jack," Laura said, recalling Jack the Ripper, who had christened himself with that moniker in one of his taunting postcards to the police.

Laura agreed to help Emily prepare Janet's house for Hank's return home. After endless hours on the phone with the insurance company Emily had learned that Hank's coverage, though not great, did at least cover the services of a part-time in-home nurse.

They arrived at the house on a cold Monday morning. Laura brought Jack, partly because she thought the bird could use a little breather from her own confined condo, and partly because she wanted to see how he would respond to his old home environment.

"I thought we'd set Hank up in the living room," Emily said. "We'll need to move some furniture. He's going to have a hospital bed, and the nurse will need space for his medications, and his physical therapy equipment."

Laura brought Jack's cage into the living room and opened the door, while she and Emily dragged furniture around. Jack watched them for a moment, then hopped out of his cage onto a side table, still not able to fully fly with his damaged wing.

"Emily, did anyone tell Hank about Janet?" Laura asked.

Emily brushed a strand of hair out of her face. "I did."

"How did he take it?"

Emily made a funny face. "I couldn't tell. His face is still pretty swollen. I know he understood me. I didn't push it. He has so many new things to adjust to."

Laura glanced around the room at the many cardboard boxes filled with Janet's things. "So does he want all of her stuff out?" she asked. "It looks like you're packing everything up."

"Just organizing," Emily said. "I don't know what to do with Janet's stuff. And Hank can't talk, so I don't know what he wants. Would you want to come home to a house filled with reminders of your dead wife?"

"I don't know."

"He didn't even get a chance to say goodbye."

She looked as if she might start crying. Laura looked away, reached into one of the open boxes, pulled out a framed photograph of Janet, holding Jack.

"You miss Mommy, Jack?" she asked.

Jack cocked his head at the picture. "*Good bird, Jack.*" He chirped. "*Good bird, Jack.*"

"Good bird, Jack," Laura repeated. She watched him carefully as he bobbed at the photograph. Jack, she was starting to realize, was much more intelligent than she had given him credit for. Animals always were. She had taught a one-armed rat to play the piano. She wondered what else this parrot was capable of. "I think he misses her," she told Emily.

"We all do," Emily said.

Laura quietly slipped out of the living room, leaving Emily and Jack alone with Janet's picture. She had never really spent much time in Janet's house. She roamed from room to room, inspecting furniture, art, trinkets, peering into the boxes Emily had filled. In the library she opened a cabinet and found a bar, shelves of high-ball and rocks glasses, mixers, strainers, even a sink. Opening an inner cabinet, she found a cache of booze: scotches, vodka, gin.

"Get me a drink," she whispered to herself.

"What are you doing?"

Emily's voice startled her. Laura turned and saw her sister holding Jack, stroking the shining green plumage on his head.

"He doesn't let me do that," Laura said.

"Have you ever tried to pet him?"

"No." Laura turned to the liquor cabinet. "I didn't know Janet was such a drinker."

"That's Hank," Emily said bitterly. "Hank likes to drink."

"*Get me a drink,*" Jack squawked.

"No kidding," Laura said.

Emily rubbed her eyes. "I found other bottles. In the bedroom, under the kitchen sink. In the bathroom."

"So *he's* the alcoholic."

Emily looked frustrated now. "Come on. We have a lot to do, and the nurse is coming tonight. There's a stack of mail in the kitchen I want to go through."

Laura closed the liquor cabinet and joined her sister in the kitchen. On the table was a small mountain range of mail, sorted into piles of bills, junk, and personal correspondence. Together the sisters sat down at the table and went through the piles. Jack stood on the table beside them. Laura handed him a magazine, which he gently accepted with his beak. He dropped the magazine on the floor. Laura picked it up and set it beside him. He stared at it for a moment, then picked it up, dropped it again.

"Laura," Emily said.

"I think he wants to play."

"Play later. If you see any insurance stuff, put it here."

Laura glanced absently through the bills. Jack continued to drop his magazine on the floor. Laura picked it up for him with one hand, sorted mail with the other.

"*Good bird, Jack.*"

"Good bird, Jack," she mumbled. One piece of mail stood out: Mutual Life Insurance Company. "Emily, what's this?"

Emily squinted at the envelope. "Insurance? Put it in the pile, we'll take a look."

"It's life insurance."

"Put it in the pile."

"*Get me a drink,*" Jack said. He cocked his head, looking for the magazine.

Laura opened the envelope from Mutual Life Insurance. It was a policy summary. "This is a policy on Janet's life," she said. "Hank is the beneficiary."

Emily nodded. "Well, I guess we'll have to help him with that too."

"Help him cash in?"

"Lots of married couples take out life insurance policies on each other. It's smart, in case something like *this* happens. Charlie and I have policies on each other."

"Oh yeah? How much money does Charlie collect if you die?"

Emily stared at her strangely. "Um, a hundred and twenty-five thousand dollars. Which is nothing, if you think about it. We have two small children-"

"Hank insured Janet's life for two and half million," Laura said.

Emily's jaw dropped and hung there like a trap door.

Laura scanned the documents again. "This policy was bought six weeks ago," she said.

Emily sighed. "Well, he's going to need it for his care."

Laura put down the insurance policy and stared at her sister, this oblivious, flustered woman. Could Emily really not see what was going on? She glanced at Jack, who was now staring fixedly at the piles of mail, his magazine either ignored or forgotten. Jack almost seemed to be eyeing the insurance policy as well.

Back at home Laura paced her condo, thinking about Janet. Jack sat on the couch, watching her, bobbing sometimes but mostly standing still, as if he could sense her agitation. Laura glanced through narrowed eyes at the hundreds of true crime volumes on her shelf. She felt as if they had betrayed her. She had read countless stories of marital debauchery, deceit, murder and revenge. And yet she felt the books had kept some secret from her, prevented her from seeing the horror story unfolding in her own sister's life.

"It doesn't make sense," she said. "Why would he be in the car? He could just as easily have been killed."

She looked at Jack, as if he might answer. "They never think that far in advance," she told herself. "They always think they'll get away with it. Of course he thought he would live. It's the perfect alibi. No one would suspect him if he was in the car."

A picture was taking shape in her head, as clear as the plot of any of her crime sagas. Her sister, a lonely, vulnerable woman, marries a man in middle age. Hank maybe sees her desperation, eagerly becomes her companion. He's been married before, a widower in fact. What happened to the first wife? Laura had no idea. And Janet doesn't know either. She doesn't know Hank at all. Turns out he's a boozehound. Get me a drink, he orders her all the time. Jack hears them, repeats what he hears.

"Ronnie," Laura whispered. Ronnie Mellman, the man Janet works with. Her secret friend. Maybe he's her real love. Maybe she wants to leave Hank to be with Ronnie. Maybe she brings him home when Hank isn't around. They have loud, passionate sex. Oh, Ronnie, oh! Jack hears them.

Repeats what he knows... to Hank? Hank figures it out because of the bird?

"What else did you see?" Laura asked the macaw. Jack stared back at her, chirped, eager to be included in conversation.

The life insurance policy. Two and a half million. That's not planning for the future, that's a fucking motive. That's revenge money. Revenge for fucking Oh Ronnie.

Laura sat down on the couch, buried her face in her hands. It was all just speculation. Circumstantial evidence. With a parrot as the only potential witness. And no proof. Hank was in the car. Would a jury believe he would risk killing himself alongside his wife? But he had survived. He was broken and crippled, but rich. And Janet was dead.

Laura reached for the framed picture of Janet and Jack. She had taken it from Janet's house, decided she wanted a memento of her sister, something she and the bird could look at when they missed Janet. She set the picture on her coffee table, reached out her arm gently toward Jack. To her surprise, he stepped onto her arm. He was surprisingly heavy. She could feel the strength of his talons. She stroked the bright green plumage of his head. He did not try to bite or claw her, and even though her mind was a hurricane, she found herself calmly smiling.

"*Good bird, Jack.*"

"Good bird, Jack." She set him on the table next to Janet's picture. "Is that what she used to tell you?" She glanced around the room for the sunflower seeds.

Jack cocked his head at the photograph. "*I'll get her,*" he screeched in a low voice.

"What did you say?" Laura asked, her voice barely above a whisper.

The macaw did not answer.

"Good bird, Jack," Laura tried.

"*I'll get her,*" Jack screeched. "*I'll get her.*"

"You'll get her," Laura repeated. "You *got* her."

Laura returned to Janet's house a few nights later, saw the nurse's car parked in the driveway. She was glad Emily wasn't there, or her mother, or anyone else. She wanted to talk to Hank face to face.

The nurse let Laura in after she explained she was Hank's sister-in-law. Laura carried Jack in his transport cage. She told the nurse she brought him by for Hank, knowing the poor man must miss not only his wife but his beloved pet as well.

"That's sweet of you, hon," the nurse said.

"Can he talk?" Laura asked.

"Not yet," the nurse replied.

In the living room Hank lay half-conscious in a hospital bed, propped up to face the television. The nurse had set up a table with medication, catheters, bed pans, spare sheets and bibs. Hank was hooked up to an IV, and once again Laura saw he had a little hand control with a square blue button, an analgesic infusion pump for administering his own medication. She crossed the room to Hank's bed and sat down, placed Jack's cage on the coffee table.

"Is he in much pain?" Laura asked.

"I would say it's pretty bad," the nurse said.

"How does this work?" Laura asked, picking up the infusion pump. "He can give himself a shot anytime he needs one?"

"Not anytime," the nurse replied. "The dosage is controlled." She lowered her voice and leaned toward Laura. "I think he's been messing with it though. I set the dosage every night before I go home. Every morning when I return I find him doped out of his mind."

"Can he do that?" Laura asked.

The nurse shrugged. "It's just a computer."

Laura thought it was probably a relatively simple operation to manipulate the infusion pump, if you knew what you were doing.

"What if he needs emergency care at night?" Laura asked. "When you're not here?"

"He has a beeper with a button he can press. It calls 9-1-1."

Laura saw the beeper resting on the table beside Hank's bed.

"I don't know if I should tell you this," Laura whispered, leaning away from Hank. "He's a drinker. There's booze all over the house. If he were to get out of bed...."

"He can't drink," the nurse said. "If he mixes alcohol with his medications, he could kill himself."

"There's a bar in the library," Laura said. "My sister found more bottles in other places. We should probably just throw everything out."

"Let's do that then," the nurse said. She stood with purpose, and Laura pointed her into the library.

She waited until she heard noises in the other room. Then she leaned toward Hank. "Hank, can you hear me? It's Laura." She shook him gently. He opened his eyes, blinked several times. She gave him a moment to orient himself.

"Can you hear me, Hank?"

Hank's head nodded minutely.

Laura leaned closer. "I know what you did to Janet, you son of a bitch. I know about the 'accident.' The insurance policy. I know about *Ronnie*."

"*Oh, Ronnie. Oh! Oh, Ronnie!*" Jack bobbed in his cage.

Hank's eyes flashed over to the bird, and Laura saw a look of pure, undisguised hatred.

"Oops," Laura whispered.

Hank turned back to her, and in his expression she saw an anger so deep it chilled her. She was grateful he was confined to a bed with two broken legs and a shattered arm.

That night Laura cried for her sister. She cried for the gentle person she never made much of an effort to get to know. She cried for the life of the innocent woman coldly usurped by a sadistic predator. She cried for her own reclusive nature, for her inability to connect with her own family. If she had ever given half a fig for anyone except herself she could have possibly prevented Janet from being murdered. If she had just seen the clues that had been right there in front of everyone's oblivious little faces, then Janet might still be alive.

For the next week Laura devoted her free time to training Jack. She removed the hand control to the infusion pump from Jack's cage, detached it from his water bottle. She opened his cage and let him out. His wing was stronger now. He could not exactly fly, but he could flap his wings and float, alighting on low surfaces such as the couch and the coffee table. Laura placed the hand control in different locations throughout the room, pointing it out to Jack, telling him to get his own drink. She watched as Jack diligently followed the controller around the room, touching the little blue button with his beak the way she had showed him. Every time he touched the blue button, she gave him a sunflower seed, until he realized that this was a fun game, and he roamed the room touching the button on his own.

When she thought he was finally ready, Laura lifted him onto her arm, fed him a handful of seeds. "Good bird, Jack," she said.

The nurse's car pulled out of Hank's driveway around ten-thirty PM. Laura parked across the street and waited. Jack bobbed in his carrier on the passenger seat. The living room window glowed with the flickering light of the television. Laura watched as the neighborhood lawn sprinklers started to turn on one by one, and decided the whicking, shicking noise would provide good cover.

She crept out of the car and slipped across the dark street, carrying Jack's cage. She knew from her visit with Emily where Janet and Hank kept the spare key to the back door, in one of the flower pots on the porch. She slid the key into the lock and crept inside.

The television cast a blue glow over Hank. His infusion pump blinked with a tiny red light. Hank lay slumped in his hospital bed, his hand upturned just a few inches from his precious blue button. A stream of drool trailed out his mouth. He looked blissfully stoned. Laura saw the emergency beeper on the table beside his bed. The table had wheels and she nudged it just beyond Hank's reach. Then she set the birdcage on the chair beside Hank's bed and opened the door.

"Get yourself a drink, Jack," she whispered, and she crept out of the living room, closing the door behind her, as Jack hopped out of his cage.

Hank heard a strange screeching noise and tried to open his eyes. His head felt like a hot cloud of cotton candy. His eyes could not focus on anything. His arm was a sandbag, immobile. Murmurs from the television bounced at him in weird delays, like echoes thrown across a canyon. Jesus Christ, how much morphine had he given himself?

There was also a strange clicking noise, and as he glacially shifted his eyeballs, he saw a blurry blue and gold shape perched on the arm of his bed. The shape bobbed rhythmically, its face bending forward, its beak tapping something. The blue button. His morphine.

The fucking bird! It was back, the demon from his nightmares. Hank felt sweat break out all over his body, itching him deep in his casts. He tried to shout at the damn thing, but could not. That fucking bird that he had hated with every fiber of his being. Janet's screeching little treasure....

Laura awoke late the next morning, to the sound of her ringing phone. The previous night came back to her in flashes- dozing in the car, running across Hank's lawn as the sun was coming up, corralling Jack back into his cage. Nodding off at a red light on the way home.

"Hello?" she mumbled into the phone. It was Emily, and she was crying again, though this time she sounded more exhausted than pained.

"You won't believe what happened, Laur," Emily sobbed.

"What?"

"Hank died last night," Emily said. "The nurse found him this morning. She said he had somehow manipulated his infusion pump to give himself more morphine."

"Is that possible?" Laura asked.

"Apparently. She said he'd been doing it every night. She even reported it to her supervisor. I feel so bad for her, Laura, she was crying."

For a moment Laura felt a dull ache of guilt in her chest, but it subsided.

"I don't know what to do," Emily said. "Now both Janet and her husband are dead."

Laura felt like she herself might actually cry, not out of guilt or remorse or fear, but because Emily, her one remaining sister, was so innocently upset.

"Would you like me to come over, Em?" Laura asked, speaking softly into the phone. "We could spend the day together. Get some coffee. Maybe go for a walk."

"I... I would really like that," Emily said.

"Let me get dressed," Laura said. "I'll be there soon."

They hung up, and Laura actually felt excited. Galvanized. She would never let anything happen to Emily, she decided. From this point on her sister would be not only her blood but her friend, her companion.

Before leaving she down beside Jack's cage. The macaw was happily playing with his rubber mouse toy, tossing it against his cage and retrieving it. Laura stroked his beautiful blue wings, teasingly pinched his smooth, hard beak.

She poured a handful of sunflower seeds into his dish.

"Good bird, Jack."

Chapter 11

The Clearing

Darren emerged from the thickly-wooded mountain path into a clearing with an old picnic table, and saw a woman sitting between two standing men. He stopped and nodded hello. He was on his way down the mountain, and these were the first hikers he had seen all day.

One of the men returned the nod. The woman looked at him. Darren immediately sensed there was something off about this trio. The men wore jeans and Timberland boots- not exactly late-August hiking attire. One was skinny and wore a white tank top with smears on it. The other was heavier, wearing a gray hoodie despite the heat. The skinny one had nodded.

The woman sat on the bench of the picnic table, the only one of the group dressed for hiking. She wore a jogging suit and trail-running shoes, carried a fanny pack and a water bottle. The wire of an iPod ran out of a band on her arm, like an I.V.

The woman's lack of a smile made Darren uneasy. Slowly he took off his backpack and set it on the ground, unzipped it and produced a bag of gorp.

"You guys going up or down?" Darren asked.

"Just restin'," said the man in the tank top.

"Hot as hell," Darren commented. He extended the bag of gorp. The group did not acknowledge it. They looked to be about his age, late-20s maybe. The men had sunken, feral faces, the pale complexions and buzzed haircuts of city boys, alley rats who hung around bars in case there was a fight. The woman, Darren thought, looked suburban. Her hiking gear was the kind purchased at an upscale athletic store. She had blondish hair pulled into a pony tail. Her amber skin glistened with sweat.

"You all from around here?" Darren asked, which immediately struck him as sort of a stupid question. It was a state park. There were no towns of any size for miles.

The woman looked at him again, then glanced down at her shoes. She looked thirsty.

"Just visitin'," said Tank Top.

The other man stared at nothing with the dead, sullen expression of a taxidermied kill. Darren got the feeling he could be standing two feet from the man, addressing him directly, and get no response. He also felt that he would not want to stand two feet from this man.

"It gets hotter higher up, where the trees thin out," Darren said. "You all heading up?"

"Maybe," Tank Top said eventually.

Darren chewed his gorp and tried not to stare. He was not oblivious, only playing dumb. He knew the way young women looked at men they knew, men with whom they had a rapport. This was not the way the woman looked now. She kept glancing between her shoes and Darren's chest, meeting his eyes in flitting dodges.

In the front pocket of his backpack there was a knife. Darren crouched down and made a show of repacking the gorp. He took a long sip from his water bottle. Quickly he fished the knife out of the backpack and slipped it into his pocket. Standing up, he realized his cell phone was in the front pocket too, and he should have grabbed that.

"Look," Darren said, standing up to his full height, which was about five-nine. "If you don't mind my asking: everything all right here?"

The woman looked into his eyes again and he clearly saw nervousness.

"We're fine, man," said Tank Top. "Just resting."

Darren pointed at the woman's feet, drawing her attention. "Twist your ankle, or something?"

"Um, no," she said.

He'd gotten her to speak at least. "What's your name?"

"Cody," she said.

A boy's name. Easy to remember.

"I'm Darren." He looked to each of the men, grinning to relax them. They did not give their names. "So where'd you all come up from?"

Cody hesitated. "I'm from Canton," she said.

"That's not far."

"I come up here to run."

Darren nodded. "You guys from Canton too?"

Hoodie said nothing. Tank Top made an impatient clicking sound with his tongue, his Timberland nudging the dirt beside the picnic table. "Nah, man," he muttered. Hoodie glanced at him, and he looked away.

Darren touched the pocket of his shorts where the knife was. He smiled at Cody. "Again, hope you don't mind my asking, Cody, but do you actually know these guys?"

For a moment it seemed somehow hotter in the clearing. Everyone looked at Darren now. Darren's mouth felt dry, and he took a drink from his water bottle to cover his quivering lips.

"I don't know them," Cody said in a low voice.

"Aw, what the fuck," Tank Top mumbled.

This was about where Darren's tough-guy movie references ran out. He had never been in a fight. Normally he was not a meddler. He came from the city, had learned to hone his indifference. He stepped back, widening his stance, dropped his arms to his sides.

"So what's going on?" he asked.

"We're just sittin' here," said Tank Top. "Mind your own fuckin' business."

"Yeah, maybe I should," Darren agreed. "But this doesn't look too legit to me."

"The fuck you gonna do about it?"

"Well," Darren said. "Maybe we don't need to do anything. Maybe I'll head on down, like I was going to, and you guys can stay, or head up. Cody, you can come with me, if you want, if you've finished your run," he said to the woman.

She looked like she wanted to stand, but she made no move to. Her eyes kept darting to the man in the hoodie.

"You should go down," said Tank Top.

Darren slowly reached down and picked up his pack, keeping all three of them in view.

"Maybe we should all go down together," he said. "It is getting late in the afternoon."

Tank Top shook his head and now Hoodie took a step forward, and pulled a nine-millimeter pistol from the front pocket of his sweatshirt.

"Get the fuck out of here," Hoodie said, his voice sounding younger than he looked.

Darren took a step backward, raising his hands. "There's no need for that, man. Come on, let's just figure this out peacefully."

Hoodie raised the gun and pointed it at Darren's face. His expression was as blank and menacing as the dark hole in the gun barrel.

Cody turned her head away. Darren saw her wipe her eyes. The men watched him, saying nothing. Darren knew this was check-mate. He would have to run down the mountain and call for help.

"All right," he said. "I don't want any trouble. I'm going."

He walked sort of sideways along the trail until he was past the clearing. Out of range of the gun, he turned and hoofed it down the trail. He had no idea how far he was from the parking lot. As he ran he pulled his backpack off and fished out his cell phone. There was no signal.

After a few minutes he stopped, turned around. An idea occurred to him. It might be hours before law enforcement showed up here in the mountains. But he could still help Cody now. He lacked a weapon that could compete with the nine-millimeter. But he still had his wits.

Darren stepped off the trail and set his backpack down next to a tree. He ran through the thick brush into the woods, maybe fifty yards, out of sight of the trail. Then he turned uphill and back-tracked toward the clearing.

The trees thinned out a little as he climbed, but he found a thick fallen trunk with an upturned spread of dirt-caked roots. Crouching behind this cover, he could see the clearing.

The woman was crying now. The men hovered over her. Hoodie held the gun against her head, and was saying something in a low mongrel voice, but Darren could not make out the words.

Darren felt around on the ground for stones, scraped a few out of the dark, upturned soil where the fallen tree's root structure had been. He picked up a good-sized rock and hurled it toward the clearing.

The rock snapped through the bushes. The two men and Cody turned their heads. Another crack of foliage ruffled nearby.

"The fuck is that?" Tank Top muttered. He turned and glanced around at the bushes, looking for an animal.

Hoodie shielded his eyes and peered into the forest. Another small crash sounded nearby. Then a rock bounced off the picnic table.

"What the fuck!?" Tank Top cried, picking a direction and shouting at it.

Darren crouched behind his cover. He could see their shapes moving around. Clearly they could not see him. He waited patiently, throwing rocks about every thirty seconds.

In the clearing Hoodie took a step toward the most recent crash, his gun pointed straight ahead.

"It must be that fucking hiker," he mumbled.

"Aw, fuck this, man, let's get outta here," Tank Top said. "He's seen us anyway. I ain't doin' any more time."

Hoodie stared into the forest for another moment. Tank Top paced the clearing. Hoodie took a step toward Cody and pressed the gun against her head.

"No, please," she said, squeezing her eyes shut.

"Don't say a fuckin' word about this," Hoodie said, and then wordlessly he and Tank Top took off, hurrying down the trail.

Darren saw them leave. He pressed himself flat against the ground. Waited several minutes for them to make their way down. Then he stood up and hustled toward the clearing. Cody was still there, he could see, still sitting at the table. Darren's mind was racing. They would probably have to bushwhack their way down. Following the trail they might run into the men again. They could hike down till they found the road, then flag down a car for help. At least Cody would be safe.

But that's not the way it went down. Darren only thought of the idea to double-back and throw stones while lying in bed later during one of his increasingly frequent sleepless nights.

Instead he had run down the mountain with his heart pounding in his chest. When he reached the parking lot he got in his car and took off, not even sure where he was going. He stopped a few miles down the road to collect himself. Took a long drink of water and tried his phone. There was still no reception and he had to drive for fifteen minutes before he got a bar.

At the police station in Canton he gave a description of the two men. The police came up with composite facial images on an imaging program on their computer.

Cody's body was found in a ravine the next day, naked, her clothes and things strewn throughout the woods. Many of her bones were broken, as if she had been pushed or dropped into the ravine.

In his mind Darren rescued her a thousand times, each escapade more harrowing and heroic than the last. In some of the rescues he even had a gun, and he drew down on the thugs like Eastwood in *The Good, The Bad, and The Ugly*. Cody even became his lover sometimes.

But movies were never thrilling in the same way for Darren again. Nor were hikes in the mountains ever as pleasant. Nor did the feelings of cowardice and impotence ever fade completely, no matter how many tales he told himself.

And the two men from the clearing were never caught.

Chapter 12

The Human Word-Processor

Stephen King sat in his office in Bangor, Maine, staring at the story he was writing on his word processor, when he realized he could not stop writing. He had written dozens of books and hundreds of short stories, and he wanted to stop-

Please God let me fucking stop

-because he had said everything he wanted to say, many times over. The ideas still poured through his mind like water coursing through the Orono Dam, but he had reached the point where he found himself drowning in the flow.

He decided his hands were to blame. As long as he had hands, he would continue to sit down at his word processor every day and churn out fresh pages. And his lifelong best friend/worst enemy, Constant Reader, would always continue to read them.

He picked up the telephone and called his neighbor, Bosco, a retired lawn mower salesman, a friend on whom he had called before for strange favors.

"Bosco, I need you to cut my hands off," said Stephen King.

"You need me to goddamn what?"

"I can't stop writing. It's killing me. I need you to cut me off. Literally."

There was a long and not-unfamiliar pause on the other end of the phone.

"Steve, maybe we should just get a six-pack and watch the Red Sox," Bosco said eventually.

"I quit drinking," said Stephen King. "I quit smoking, I quit drugs. But I'm addicted to writing. It's like a rat burrowing inside me, eating me alive."

"That sounds like one of your stories right there."

It was. The story he was working on was called "The Rat," about a writer whose latest story had taken on the literal form of a rat with sharp teeth, and was burrowing into the writer's stomach, growing, soon to consume him, or maybe just cause him to burst and spill his guts all over the floor like spaghetti and meatballs.

"If you're refusing to help me, then I may have to take matters into my own hands," said Stephen King.

"Come on over and watch the game," said Bosco.

Stephen King did not go over to Bosco's to watch the Sox. Instead he picked up a meat cleaver from his kitchen with his left hand and used it to hack off his right hand. He stared at the blood-gushing stump in terror and called 9-1-1 on his cell phone with his remaining hand.

Stephen King knew enough about human anatomy to know that a person could not use a cleaver to cut off both of their hands. Because once you cut off the first one....

So he self-amputated the second hand with a revolving table saw in his garage. By the time the ambulance arrived he was sitting on his front porch with his arms in the air, light-headed and mumbling incoherently from blood loss.

For a couple of months he was happy. He had no hands, and thus no fingers, and thus could not continue to write, and finally he was able to fucking relax. He had saved the hands in zip-locked plastic bags in his freezer, which had begun to disturb his wife.

But as time went on he knew that he would not be able to quit writing until he completed the rat story. Unfinished business was worse than addiction. Soon he was back in his office, having affixed to the stump of one wrist a prosthetic device that could hold a pencil. To his other wrist-stump he had affixed a prosthetic device that held a pencil-sharpener. At first it was slow-going and physically awkward to write, but soon the pages flew off his table. He then discovered it was easier just to affix two unsharpened pencils to his wrist-stumps and type the story on his word processor, pecking away like a bird with long talons.

But the self-loathing and anxiety of addiction returned, and he knew that the rat story was indeed a vicious rat, literally (well, figuratively) eating his soul. He realized the problem was that his arms were still capable of working a word processor. His goddamn fucking arms.

The next day he waited until Bosco had left his house to go bowling with some friends, then he dialed his neighbor's number and left a message on his voicemail: "Bosco, old boy, I'm really, truly sorry for what I'm going to do today. I owe you a six-pack of cold ones."

The yard behind Bosco's house contained all different models of lawn mowers, both push- and ride-, as Bosco, though retired from sales, liked to keep his hand in the lawn-mowing game around Bangor. Stephen King walked next door and selected a sizable Husqvarna push-model and yanked the chord with his teeth. The mower roared to life. Stephen King then pushed the mower over onto its side with his feet, and knelt on the grass before the hungry, gyrating blade.

"This is for the greater good," he told himself. He closed his eyes, held out his arms, and leaned forward.

Bosco and his wife spent the rest of the summer spraying their back yard with a hose to clean all of Stephen King's blood out of the grass. But the promised six-pack arrived on Bosco's doorstep. Bosco knew his neighbor to be a bit of an eccentric. Soon they were back to watching baseball together, though Stephen King was unable to clap when the Sox scored a run because the stumps of his arms were about five and eight inches long, respectively.

There was no more writing, and no more rat, and Stephen King felt happy for a while. But then the baseball season ended, leaving many slow nights with not much to do, and inevitably he found himself back in his office, staring at his word processor. The beast had drawn him back. The rat had filled his intestines, devoured his stomach, was chewing and hacking its way upward through his torso toward his heart. Only one entity would survive, he knew- either the rat, or his soul. He must finish the story, give birth to the rat, purge himself of the monster.

Pretty much anything could be found on the internet. Stephen King scanned the web late at night until he discovered a revolutionary new technology being developed in Korea. Though the device was not on the market yet, Stephen King was able to purchase a prototype using his fame, the fine art of persuasion, and his television royalties from *Under the Dome*.

In two weeks a package arrived in the mail. The package contained a long, rolled-up mat, which Stephen King kicked open with his feet and spread across his office floor. The mat was a life-sized replica of a keyboard that a person could type with stepping from one letter or symbol to the next, like the board game *Twister*. Stephen King paid a grad student at the University of Maine $200 and a case of brews to hook up the mat to his word processor.

Stephen King was back in business. It took him a couple of weeks to master the new technology, but soon he was step-typing like a wizard. He could hop out fifty-six words a minute, almost twenty pages a day, before collapsing each afternoon, exhausted, into a well-deserved nap. He developed such strong legs and nimble feet that he ran the Bangor marathon, and finished fourth. His grandchildren came over to play *Dance, Dance Revolution*, and he destroyed them at it. And the manuscript of "The Rat" swelled to 784 pages. He edited it down to 690 by stomping on the "delete" button, then he kicked the story off to his publisher.

"The Rat" was a complex piece of meta-horror-fiction filled with long chapters wherein the writer converses with the rat inside him, begs for his life, grants the rat freedom, in the form of a novel, in exchange for his own (the writer's) spiritual freedom. The book sold four million copies, and critics called it the most important philosophical work since Kafka's *Metamorphosis*.

Three re-prints and an HBO miniseries later, Stephen King found himself back in his office, miserably kicking out "The Rat 2." He felt worse than ever, a slave to Constant Reader, who loved "The Rat," and wanted more.

"I can't take it anymore, Bosco," he told his neighbor. "I need you to take your chainsaw and cut off my legs."

"Steve, you know I can't do that," Bosco said.

"No one else will help me."

"There's liability, old buckaroo."

"I'll pay you! I'll sign a waiver with my toes!"

"Nope. Sorry."

Stephen King knew he could not cut off his legs on his own. With no arms he had nothing with which to operate a tool. But what he did have was a familiarity with the local train schedule.

On a dry fall night he staggered out to the train tracks on the edge of town. If he could not step on the typing mat, he could not continue writing, and "The Rat 2" would be forced to leave him alone. He would live out the rest of his days in a comfortable chair, maybe one of those dangling door-seats that babies used. He could bounce in the doorway and watch the Sox. No more goddamn fucking writing.

His chest swelled with relief as he lay down on the cold ground, his legs straddling the railroad tracks. Soon he heard the faint roar of the approaching train. The roar grew louder. He closed his eyes. There was a loud blast from the train's horn. The blast became a wail. He felt the wind blow back his hair as the train deftly severed his legs just below the waist, churning the blood-spurting appendages into sausage.

"I have finally retired from writing," Stephen King told his family and friends, from the sterile comfort of a mechanical hospital bed. "This time I'm serious."

He sat up in bed at the ICU and finally began to enjoy his life. He watched TV, listened to music, was spoon-fed apple sauce and soup by attractive nurses, and read books propped up on a tray table beneath his chin, turning the pages with his tongue.

Bosco visited and they watched the Red Sox. There were no more demons tormenting Stephen King.

Until the rat returned, rousing him from sleep in the dead of night, pregnant with fresh ideas, gnawing at his brain. Gnawing. Gnawing and gnawing with its pointed yellow teeth.

Teeth. Yes. He still had his teeth. He could still battle the rat as long as he had his teeth.

His nurse, a slender blonde named Veronica, arrived to check on him in the morning.

"What would you like for breakfast, Mr. King?" Veronica asked. "More oatmeal with blueberries?"

"You know what I feel like, Veronica?" said Stephen King. "I feel like eating something sharp and delicious. Could you bring me a block of cheese?"

"Cheese?"

"The biggest block of cheese you can find! The one all the way in the back of the cooler!"

"All right, Mr. King...."

Veronica was used to unusual requests from her patients, and she knew this particular patient to be more unusual than usual. In half an hour she returned from the hospital cafeteria with a brick of orange cheddar the size of a shoebox.

"Let me get you a knife and fork," she said.

"You know what?" said Stephen King, a feeling of perverse enjoyment rising within him. "Just drop it on my tray here and push the tray toward my face. I really feel like chomping this motherfucker down. Might just gnaw on it all day."

"All right, Mr. King...."

Veronica set the cheese down on Stephen King's tray table and nudged the tray toward his mouth. Her patient licked his lips and leaned forward.

When Veronica returned later to check Stephen King's vitals, she found the author asleep, s satisfied grin on his face. Curiously she peered down at the block of cheese. He had not eaten it. Instead it looked like he had simply chewed it, or bitten it rather, in what became clear as an oddly specific pattern. She leaned forward to look more closely. Stephen King had used his teeth to hack and bite jagged words into the cheese. She read aloud:

"Chapter One: The rat crawled out of his belly and began chewing his brain."

"How do you like it?"

"Oh my God!" Her hand flew to her chest. She stumbled backward into his heart monitor. "You scared me."

"Sometimes I scare myself," he said. He grinned at her, his teeth caked with orange gobs. "Veronica," said Stephen King. "I need more cheese."

Chapter 13

Toesies

Henry and Kylie stopped their game of Monopoly as their grandfather limped into the living room. Henry, about to roll, gripped the dice in a quivering hand. For a moment the cherry red hotels and conifer green houses on the board became a derelict plastic ghost town. The scraping of Grampa's foot on the wood floor sounded like the lurch of some desert creature, hobbling toward them across the dusty salt flats.

Grampa sat down in his chair by the fireplace with a loud exhalation of breath. He stared at the game.

"Who's winning?" he asked.

"I am," Kylie said. Though Henry had a taller stack of money in front of him, she had more properties, including hotels on the Oranges.

Henry could not take his eyes off his grandfather's foot. Whenever Grampa entered a room Henry was frozen by the strange dead appendage, a mystery concealed in an old brown shoe. The dice slipped from his hands, as if escaping, and their clatter against the board brought him back to the game.

"Oh no," he said, as he advanced his battleship token to Atlantic Avenue, where Kylie had three houses.

"Eight hundred dollars!" Kylie cried.

Henry grudgingly handed over the money, more than half of his loot. His sister invested the money in a fresh round of houses on the Greens.

Grampa sat in his chair and tapped his twisted foot. "She's gotcha on the ropes there, boy."

In the kitchen they could hear their parents preparing dinner. On his next roll Henry landed on Pennsylvania Avenue, also his sister's territory, and was forced to liquidate his assets. Neither he nor Kylie ever surrendered in the face of bankruptcy. They always played the game to the last devastating roll, like gamblers at the craps table. In a few moments Kylie had all the money and was counting it gloatingly as Henry stared at a white row of mortgaged properties.

Kylie, gripping a fistful of Monopoly dollars, took a victory lap around the board with her car token, passing her skyline of properties.

"You're a real tycoon," Grampa said.

Kylie smiled. Henry glanced toward the kitchen to make sure his parents were out of sight and out of the range of hearing. Then he leaned toward his grandfather.

"Grampa, what happened to your foot?" he asked.

The victorious grin on Kylie's face disappeared. Grampa tapped his foot on the floor, a bass drum thump beneath the snare crackle of the fire.

"I lost my toesies," Grampa said.

"What are toesies?" Kylie asked.

Grampa leaned down and pinched one of her tiny pink socks. "These are toesies."

Kylie giggled. Henry stared at his grandfather's shoe. Was there really just a stump of a foot in there, with no toes? "How did you lose them?" Henry asked.

"That's a scary story," Grampa said.

"I like scary stories," said Henry.

Grampa leaned back in his chair and grinned down at the children. "All right," he said. "When I was a boy I lived on a farm out in Heath. That's way out west, near the Vermont border. Our nearest neighbors were three miles away. The nights were black as pitch and quiet as the inside of a dead man's skull."

Henry looked at his grandfather's face and imagined a gleaming skeleton, a fleshless grinning rock with black eye sockets.

"The nights were cold out there on the farm," Grampa said. "We heated the farmhouse with a woodstove, but in winter, it would get real cold up in my bedroom. No heat. Just me and my blanket. I always kept my blanket wrapped around my feet. Didn't want to freeze my little toesies off."

He pinched Kylie's toes again, making her squirm and giggle.

"But one night," Grampa said, his voice now just above a whisper. "The blanket slipped off."

His foot began to tap and Henry imagined Grampa's toes turning to icicles, frozen blue nuggets that snapped and dropped off.

"At first I only felt a tickle," Grampa said. "I was still half-asleep. Just a little tickle, like the wind, or a cold draft whispering through a crack in the window. But then I felt a nibble."

Henry's feet curled involuntarily beneath his legs. Kylie rubbed her pink socks with both hands.

"I thought maybe it was a mouse," Grampa said. "Nipping at my toes. So I opened my eyes and peered down across my blankets. And do you know what I saw?"

Henry and Kylie glanced at each other, shaking their heads.

"A little man with a tangled red beard, standing there at the end of the bed. Smiling at me with his dirty, chipped, yellow teeth. Tufts of hair sprouting from his ears. The moonlight gleaming in his eyes. His breath stank like a dead pig. And my foot was in his mouth."

Kylie moved around the Monopoly board and sat so close to Henry that they were touching. Henry inched away from his sister, to show his grandfather he was not afraid.

"'Mmm,' the little man said. 'Toesies.' And then he bit me."

"Grampa," Kylie whimpered.

Henry's mouth was dry. He opened it to protest, but could find no words.

"By the time I screamed and ran out of my bed my toes were gone," Grampa said. "He got all five of them right off my foot. Crunched them up with his teeth and swallowed them. Then he disappeared."

Grampa leaned back toward the fire, his lame foot now rubbing a soft circle on the floor.

"Did that really happen?" Henry asked.

Their father walked into the room holding a glass of wine.

"You guys playing Monopoly?" he asked.

"We were just talking," Grampa said.

"Talking about what?"

"I was telling them how I lost my toes."

"That's great, Dad. You told them about the tractor. Kids, you listen to your grandfather. Farm machinery can be dangerous. You can lose a limb."

Henry frowned at his father, then at his grandfather.

"Dinner in five minutes," their father said, and he went back into the kitchen.

"Grampa, did a tractor run over your foot?" Henry asked.

"It was no tractor," said his grandfather. "Look at this."

Henry and Kylie watched as Grampa pulled off his leather shoe. Underneath he wore a faded brown sock with holes in the sole. Grampa grunted and bent over, rolling the sock slowly down from his ankle and over his flaky yellow foot. When he pulled the sock away they saw the mangled appendage. Instead of toes Grampa had five pinkish stumps of various lengths, the tissue bristling with twisted purple veins.

"A tractor would have only flattened them," Grampa said. "But my toes were bitten clean off. See? That's what a strong bite does to you. Rips your toesies right off."

Henry's mouth hung open and Kylie looked like she was about to cry. Grampa carefully pulled his sock back on and reached for his shoe.

"Dinner!" their father called from the kitchen.

That night Henry had trouble falling asleep. He lay under the covers in the dark, staring up at the ceiling. Only a thin shaft of moonlight lit the room. Before bed he had checked the closet and under the bed, the usual hiding places of unpleasant things. He had leaned his hockey stick up against his bedside table, in case he needed to slash something during the night.

He did not know when he drifted off, but he awoke in the dark to the sound of his door creaking open. He curled his feet and legs up to his body and reached for his hockey stick.

"Henry?"

It was Kylie.

"What?"

"Are you asleep?"

"Obviously not, I'm talking to you."

He stared at her dark shape in the doorway.

"Can I sleep with you?" she asked.

"No. Why?"

"Something was touching my foot."

Henry sat up in bed and turned on his lamp. Kylie stood in her pajamas, rubbing her eyes. He put down his hockey stick. "You're just scared from Grampa's story."

"It was wet."

"What was wet?"

"The thing touching my foot."

In his room, with the light on, surrounded by his things, Henry felt bolstered by their two-year difference in age. Kylie was younger than him, and she had beaten him at Monopoly, and he thought about banishing her back to her dark room. That would teach her to gloat after taking all his money and property. But the truth was he liked it when she slept with him. Her body was small but warm, and she smelled funny in a pleasant way, and she held onto his arm in her sleep.

"All right," he said. "Get in."

She padded across the carpet and hopped into the bed. He waited until she was beneath the covers, then turned off the light. She curled up beside him and gripped his arm.

Henry felt her hot breath on his cheek. He lay back against his pillow and tried to sleep.

"Why do you think something was touching your feet?" he asked eventually.

"I felt it," she replied.

"Were you dreaming?"

"If I was dreaming, it wouldn't be wet."

Henry took a deep breath. A tractor had run over Grampa's foot. Dad had said so. Hadn't he? What exactly had been said?

He was not sure if it was the cold that woke him later, or the slight tugging sensation on his foot. Suddenly Henry was bolt awake. His blankets were gone from the bottom of his bed, his bare feet exposed to the night air. And something was wet.

"Kylie-"

Kylie murmured beside him, her little hands clenching his arm.

Henry stared down across his body to the foot of his bed. In the sliver of moonlight he saw the withered face of his grandfather, hunched over the bed. His grandfather was grinning, and laughing softly under his breath.

And Henry's foot was in his mouth.

"Grampa?"

His voice came out like chalk powder, barely a whisper. He felt the gnarled bark of his grandfather's teeth on his toes, the slimy wet eel of his tongue.

"Grampa, what are you doing?"

Kylie squirmed but did not wake up. Henry reached for his hockey stick.

"Mmm," Grampa muttered, his mouth smiling around Henry's foot. "Toesies."

And then he bit down hard.

Acknowledgements

Many of these stories appeared previously in the following publications: "Watch City" in *Infernal Ink*; "Scream Queen" and "Mercy Kill" in *Crack the Spine*; "Sertraline Dreams" and "The Clearing" in *The Indiana Voice Journal*; "A Dark North Territory" in *Pilcrow and Dagger*; "Coyotes" in *The Crime Factory*; "Effigy" in *Rathalla Review*; "Just the Usual Horses" in *The Oddville Press*; "The Human Word-Processor" in *Wilderness House Literary Review*; "Toesies" in *Morpheus Tales*. The author wishes to thank the editors of these publications for their generous support.

Adam Matson's fiction has appeared internationally in over twenty magazines and journals. He is the author of the short story collection *Sometimes Things Go Horribly Wrong*. He lives in Portland, Oregon.

CPSIA information can be obtained
at www.ICGtesting.com
Printed in the USA
JSHW020015280421
14042JS00005B/138

9 781087 870151